JULES

MOONRISE
BOOK
2

NIGHT IS FOR HUNTING

NIGHT IS FOR HUNTING

JULES KELLEY

NIGHT IS FOR HUNTING
Moonrise, Book 2

CITY OWL PRESS
www.cityowlpress.com

Cover Design by MiblArt. All stock photos licensed appropriately.

Edited by Tee Tate.

For information on subsidiary rights, please contact the publisher at info@cityowlpress.com.

Print Edition ISBN: 978-1-64898-248-4

Digital Edition ISBN: 978-1-64898-249-1

Printed in the United States of America

"And remember the night is for hunting, and forget not the day is for sleep."

– Rudyard Kipling

PROLOGUE

No matter how many times Val Kunes cleared the text message notification from his phone, it kept showing back up. Not that he needed the reminder; he knew what it said without looking. He could see it every morning when he closed his eyes and every evening when twilight fell, making it finally safe to peel back the light-blocking curtains on his windows. It haunted him, waking and sleeping. Vampires didn't dream, but this nightmare followed him everywhere.

Happy early anniversary, babe. Took me ages to find this number. Been thinking about you lately. The Strip can't compare to the Castro in the 80s, but there are some sweet young things to ease the pain of you getting away. Think I might finally find your replacement, just in time for consummation on Halloween. Kisses!

His phone pinged in his lap—the notification popping up again probably—but he didn't look down at it. Not that he could've seen it anyway; opening his eyes more than a sliver was asking for a migraine. His sunglasses were the biggest pair he could find online and covered most of his face, but the sky was still glowing orange, the sun just barely below the mountaintops. Night was falling, but not fast enough.

He hadn't seen this much natural light in years. Maybe not since 1983. His skin itched, and he couldn't tell if it was the effect of the diffused, fading sunlight or if it was just his imagination. He scratched idly at his wrist, remembering the red, blistering boils that had blossomed there so long ago on Castro Street, the tightening panic in his stomach that he'd been infected. That he'd been cursed. That the gay cancer had found him, just like it had found so many of his friends. Just like it would eventually find Don and Jim and Solomon.

The once-unfamiliar ache in his stomach was as vivid as the memory of vomiting up blood when he'd tried to eat the tsoureki from his father's bakery to soothe it. He remembered curling up on his mattress in his one-room apartment, the door locked, the curtains pulled, and sobbing in terror and pain and guilt that he was going to die and leave his parents alone without their only son.

"You could get back in the trunk." Diego's voice broke into his memories. "Sleep a while longer."

Val blinked, coming back to the present, the ghost of crippling hunger and raw terror still in his belly, the memory of his old sun-drenched apartment slipping away into the gathering shadows. Diego was in the driver's seat, eyes glued to the road, both hands on the Audi's leather steering wheel like a good little werewolf valet with no respect for speed limits—exactly the reason Val had gone to him for help.

Val shook his head. "I'll be fine. We shouldn't stop again unless we have to."

They were on a deadline. Halloween was in a week, which meant he had seven days to find the vampire who had ruined his life and stop him from ruining someone else's. Well. Seven *nights*. And it started with the one they were driving into.

CHAPTER ONE

"THE THING IS, WE'RE NOT WOLVES." HALEY FERN FOLDED HER HANDS behind her head, the cool grass slowly warming to her body and emitting a sweet scent that tickled her sensitive nose, mingling with the scents of pondwater, algae, and aftershave. "We're humans who turn *into* wolves, but all except the brand-new shifters still have their human mind. We have wolfish impulses, sure, and they're stronger when we're shifted, but we can still override them. It's not like we don't know any better."

Leland hummed, just a hint of a noise to let her know he was still listening. She took a deep breath and continued.

"So, Diego, for example, could use the *I didn't know what I was doing* defense because he was still in the new-wolf stage, but I'll go alpha on the whole tribunal if they let Sharon Allen and her butthole boyfriend—excuse my French—use it."

She could only just see the blue-checked plaid shoulder of Leland Sommers's flannel shirt from where she was sprawled, but she could hear his soft, amused snort and then the hesitation of breath that told her he was debating his response. Either that or he thought there might be a fish on the other end of his fishing line. A soft *bloop* as the bobber went under revealed it was the latter. He didn't start reeling it in, though, so it must've been just a nibble.

And wow, didn't that sound good? A little nibble, either of Leland or of the damn fish he hadn't even caught yet. The full moon being just a week away meant that her appetites—for both food and sex—were running hot. At least so far, nothing had set off her temper; the cranky moons were the worst.

"I'm still trying to wrap my head around the whole thing," Leland admitted after a long moment, yanking Haley back to the topic at hand. "I know it's been almost six months, but sometimes I'll be sitting at the desk at work and thinking I hallucinated the whole thing. Like a really weird stress dream."

"To be fair, it was really weird for me too, and I've been a werewolf my whole life." A werewolf, sure, but part of a pack—first in Pine Grove, and then when she was in college in Seattle—that respected the laws of the community and at least didn't openly hate humans. Heck, the Pine Grove pack was so mixed she couldn't think of more than a handful of all-wolf families. Most of them were married to humans and had a combination of human and werewolf children. Her brush with violent werewolf supremacists back in the spring had been shocking and unsettling for her too—and the fact that the offenders' hearing was coming up, and she'd be expected to give testimony, was a looming shadow at the back of her mind.

It could wait until next week, though. A full moon on Halloween in a town where her pack of werewolves was the main tourist attraction was enough stress for now.

Let it go, Haley. That's why you're out here on a fishing break with your new boyfriend. To forget about all of that for an hour or two.

Except that Leland would have been content to sit and fish for hours without saying a word, and Haley was thirty more seconds of intense boredom away from shifting into wolf form and zooming around the field just for something to do, so "forgetting" wasn't going very well.

"You said that's not for another month or so, right? November, December?" Leland said, and Haley sighed.

"Yeah." She tugged her sleeves down over her hands as she stared up at the afternoon sky and laughed wryly. "If we survive Halloween."

"Mm." Leland finally set aside the fishing rod, resting it on the forked stick he had stuck into the wet soil at the edge of the lake for that purpose. "Tell me about Halloween." He turned toward her, arms propped on his knees, and Haley stared at his rough hands, thinking about what they felt like on her body. When she didn't answer after a moment, Leland prodded, "What do I need to be prepared for?"

Haley snorted. That was a loaded question. "For me to need five pizzas and a six pack to myself afterward," she muttered. "No, but seriously. Halloween is a big deal for the local businesses. The tourist traffic we get over the week is usually enough to put just about everybody in the black for the rest of the year—the B&B, the diner, the motel..." She swallowed, guilt trickling in as it did almost every time she thought about it. "We... Last year, I had been officially alpha for only about a month, and everyone decided to play it more low-key."

Leland nodded. "Understandable. Don't want to have a bunch of out-of-towners milling around when you're still getting your bearings."

Haley glanced away from him, watching the clouds scutter across the deep blue October sky. "Yeah," she agreed. "Anyway. Everyone has kind of been living lean because of it, so this year I...I took out a couple of ads, on the internet and in some papers." With her own money, actually, not from the pack fund. Her private apology for being the reason for the mediocre year before.

"I'll be around to be sure it doesn't get out of hand if a bunch of people show up," Leland promised immediately. "Hell, I'll even call George and get some tips."

Haley couldn't help a soft smile, and she held one hand out to invite him closer. "I hope there's enough people to give you something to do," she admitted. *I hope it's not a bust, like last year.*

"If nothing else, I'm sure Diego will get into something," Leland joked with a crooked smile.

"Hopefully, the fact that he can't help being a wolf will keep him out of the worst trouble." Haley laughed. "He's starting to keep a sense of self when shifted, but at this stage, it'll be kind of hazy for him. Like when you're dreaming, but you know you're dreaming."

"And you think that'll make him more or less trouble?"

"Oh, who knows. But at least he'll be working on mostly animal instinct, which is a little more predictable. He doesn't have the best track record for following the rules when he's human."

"Who, Diego?" Leland drawled flatly. "Surely you're not thinking of the same person I am."

"No, no, of course not. He'd never do anything like spend the night at the vampire colony we technically still aren't allowed to set foot in." She rolled her eyes. "But they seem to like him. Haven't murdered him yet anyway."

Leland chuckled, but the bobber on his fishing line went under, the line spooling out, and he started a patient sweep-and-reel motion that he'd told her made the fish less likely to escape. Haley sat up, interested now that there was finally some action, but her thoughts still drifted to all the other things she *should* be doing. Was she forgetting something? Her mom had always seemed to be endlessly busy the week before Halloween, but by the time Haley had been old enough to start helping out with major tasks, Kimberly had seemed determined to keep Haley out of the loop. She'd stopped bringing Haley to alpha meetups, didn't talk to her about anything more than the most surface issues. Haley had learned to stop asking.

The tension in the fishing line went slack suddenly, and Leland huffed as he reeled it in, the hook empty of either bait or fish. He set it to the side, then dug a bottle of hand sanitizer out of his backpack. The sharp alcohol scent prickled Haley's nose, centering her in the present.

"You know," Leland said, shaking his hands out, "if that worry line on your forehead gets any deeper, we could put up a sign and charge admission to the Grand Canyon." She snorted, and he grinned, clearly pleased with himself. "You need a distraction, Fern?"

Oh, heck yes. Butterflies thrilled to life in her stomach, and she flopped back into the grass. "God, please distract me," she laughed.

Leland stretched out beside her and braced himself on one elbow, dancing his other hand up her ribs until she giggled, ticklish and eager.

"Then again, you probably have a lot of important things that I shouldn't be keeping you from." The scrape of his stubble across her neck was a welcome delight, and the soft press of his lips to her jaw sent a shiver dancing down her spine. It was still a novelty to have him touching her like this without doubt or guilt clouding her emotions, and usually she was on board with taking their time to savor the sensations. Leland didn't like to rush things, which was fine most of the time, but not today.

"Pick up the pace, Sommers," she laughed as his touch stayed above her shirt, though he did tease over the side of her breast. "I've got almost six months of sexual frustration to get out of my system."

"Six months, huh?" His eyebrows went up, but he curved his palm around her breast, rubbing the heel of his hand over her nipple. "Are you trying to say you wanted to jump me the first day we met?"

"By day two, at the very least." She huffed impatiently, arching her back to look for more pressure, and he grinned as he popped open the first three buttons on her flannel, to the center of her chest, and slipped his hand inside.

"Well, it was day one for me," he murmured, nipping soft kisses down the side of her neck toward her chest. "And every day since."

"Sweet talker," she gasped accusingly, twisting to encourage the movement. "You know you don't have to impress me to get in my pants, right?"

Leland just laughed against her skin, the rumble of it sinking past her breastbone and warming her all the way to her core. Jeez, how were they not naked yet?

He'd just gotten around to tugging her bra cup down and finally, *finally* wrapping that lovely tongue around her nipple when her phone rang from the grass beside her. She fumbled for it, slapping at the Send to Voicemail prompt on the screen, and sighed as Leland worked his way over to her other breast.

Two seconds later, it rang again.

This time, she actually read the screen, and she frowned when she saw Michele's name. *Crap.* This was probably an emergency. Michele didn't like talking on the phone and would text her unless it was urgent.

"Hang on," she said, two of the most difficult words she'd ever uttered. "I need to take this."

Leland sat back, and Haley took a moment to steady her breathing and tamp down her sharp annoyance before she answered.

"Sorry," Michele said as soon as Haley said hello. "I don't think I'm going to be back by Halloween. The VA said there's been a complication with getting my uncle's home health aide, and they're not going to have it straightened out for a week or so. He can't take care of himself for more than a day or two at a time, so..."

"Oh." Haley knew better than to ask if Michele would be all right on her own for the full moon; that woman had gone through more than Haley could even imagine. But there was one thing... "What about Diego? Do I need to go get him?"

On her other side, she saw Leland suddenly tune in. Diego had gotten permission to go up to Ashton for a "wakeover" with his vampire friend, but she was sure he had to be wearing out his welcome. Most of the coven tolerated his presence for short periods of time, but even the more generous among them weren't in a hurry to have a long-term werewolf around the parts.

Michele snorted. "Believe it or not, apparently he's staying longer. I texted him about it a minute ago, and he said he'd call you when he needed to come home."

The back of her neck tingled; that seemed too easy. Her mother would've said it was the "alpha sense." Something deep in her gut insisted that someone, somewhere wasn't telling her the whole truth. And knowing the people involved, that someone was probably Diego.

But she shoved it aside; that wasn't fair to Diego. She had no proof. Maybe they were just having a great time playing video games or watching movies or making out. Heck, maybe he was getting laid and was just being cagey about it. She'd lied more than once about sneaking out with a beau when she was a teenager. And anyway, Leonard had no problem calling her to retrieve her wayward pup if he got tired of babysitting by proxy.

No sooner had she thought it than her phone beeped with an incoming call. *Speak of the devil.*

"Well, I guess I ought to thank him. Redrafting the treaty isn't nearly so awkward now that they have to be nice to at least one of us."

"Silver linings, right?" Michele said wryly. "Anyway, I'll let you know if anything changes."

"Thanks, Michele. I hope it all turns out."

Leland was looking at her with bright amusement as she ended the call. "Did I hear that right? Diego is playing hooky with the vampires?"

"Yep." She shook her head as she pulled up her missed calls. "I keep feeling like I ought to be worried about him, but..."

She trailed off as she read the name at the top of the list once, twice, again. *Crap.* What she wouldn't give to go back to five seconds ago, when she'd thought the grumpy vampire lord at the top of the mountain was calling to berate her over her most headstrong, wayward pack member.

It would have been better than seeing *Mom* in big green letters.

A voicemail notification popped up as she stared at her screen, and she tapped the icon with a shaking finger as she got her bra and sweater back in place with the other hand. It felt wrong to be listening to her mother's voice with her boobs hanging out.

"Hi, sweetie. I was just calling to let you know I'll be in town soon. I thought it might be nice to see each other for Halloween. Just me. Dennis is staying here." There was a brief pause, a small laugh that sounded tight and nervous on the recording. *"Anyway, I can file the official paperwork if you want me to, but I thought it might be okay for this to be more informal. See you soon!"*

The message ended, and Haley sat stone-still, staring at the gentle ripples of dragonflies landing on the pond, her mind whirring faster than their wings. Of course, she wouldn't make her own mother fill out the non-pack-member permissions for being in pack territory; the woman had been the alpha of these wolves most of Haley's life, after all.

But was that a test? Was she checking to see if Haley was running things correctly? And why in the heck was she coming to Pine Grove anyway? Maybe things weren't going well with her new man, if she was leaving him in Ohio for this trip. Or what if Julio had told her Haley hadn't been able to handle the infiltration and attempted overthrow of her pack? Haley had downplayed everything when she'd told Kimberly about it.

When she finally registered Leland's voice beside her, it was clear he'd already called her name more than once.

"Fern? Haley, you okay? Was it Diego?"

"No, it—" She shook herself and put on a quick smile for his benefit. "It wasn't Diego." *Great timing, though, showing up just when I've lost my newest pack member. Again.* "It was my mom. She's...she's coming to visit."

CHAPTER TWO

DIEGO'S FAVORITE THING ABOUT DRIVING FAST WAS HOW EASY IT WAS to feel like he was leaving things behind. As if Montana fading in his rearview mirror was taking with it the nightmare he'd been living in since May. Every mile marker that zipped past as he wove between the cars on the interstate, every shift in the landscape, was a little more space between himself and the horror of full moons, tracking collars, and the reflexive sensation of pure terror whenever he heard a wolf howl.

But then again, beside him in the passenger's seat was a vampire sipping blood out of a fucking juice box, so maybe he wasn't leaving as much behind as he thought. But it wasn't like he could afford to replace his totaled BMW and drive back home to Vegas on his own, so he'd deal with it.

Home. His skin tingled with the thought. He understood why he wasn't allowed to contact his family, understood the danger it would put them in, but he'd been gone from Vegas for several months even before his life had been turned upside down. He'd been staying with his cousin in Spokane for at least a year by the time he took that fateful drive into the wilds of western Montana. And now he was officially a missing person.

His whole family probably thought he was dead. Fuck, his birthday and Día de Muertos was in a week. Would they have a picture of him on the ofrenda? *Shit.* That thought made his chest ache so sharply he felt it in his teeth.

No. Better to focus on why they were really going and not let himself get sidetracked by the thought of his family. Besides, they were only going to be there one, maybe two nights. It would hurt worse to see them for that little time and have them ripped away again. He cleared his throat.

"When's this vampire guy expecting us? And what's his title, anyway? Prince, king...?"

Val laughed softly. "He's an archon. A high-ranking mediator, essentially. And he...isn't expecting us."

"Um." Diego risked a quick glance at Val, who was staring out the window. He'd taken his sunglasses off once night fell but had pushed them up into his wavy, dark hair, giving him a rakish look and setting off his sharp jaw. Not that Diego had time to get more than a glimpse while weaving between cars on the freeway at ninety-plus miles an hour. "If he's such a big deal, shouldn't we have an appointment or something?"

And hopefully this archon fucker was just a mediator for vampires and didn't give a shit about werewolves, because Diego *really* needed the Las Vegas pack to not know he was in town without proper permissions.

"He doesn't take appointments." Diego could feel the tension radiating off Val's body from across the car. "Once every few months, he opens to public hearings. If his advisors think your case is worthy, they'll bring you in to speak with him."

"That's some medieval shit," Diego grumbled. "All right, but you've got a good case. Or—not *good*, but important."

Val made a frustrated noise. "I hope he thinks so."

Nothing else was forthcoming, and Diego didn't prompt him, sitting with the uncomfortable silence. He owed Val that much. Val had vouched for Diego back in the spring when Diego had accidentally wandered into the abandoned ski resort that the local vampire community had claimed as their own, keeping the lord of the colony from punishing him or Haley's pack. Since then, he and Val had kept in contact through text messages and not-quite-allowed late-night meetings and had developed something of a friendship.

So, when Val had asked to talk in person about two weeks ago, Diego had driven Michele's truck up to the faded *Ashton Family Ski Resort* sign at the boundary of the colony's territory. Val had climbed into the cab of the pickup and turned to him with a haunted look.

"Remember how I told you I knew what it was like to be turned without consent?" he'd said, and Diego hadn't been able to keep from looking directly at the healed bite marks on Val's neck, his own scarred shoulder throbbing in sympathy. *"Well, the vampire who turned me has resurfaced. He's attacking people again. I need your help."*

And that was how Diego found himself driving as fast as possible from Pine Grove, Montana, to Las Vegas, Nevada, to try to make the usually fourteen-hour trip in one night, before sunrise. Thank fuck at least the nights were longer in late October.

"Archons are typically very old," Val said now. "And many of them still cling to their ideas from when they were alive, which can be very different from modern ideas of justice." He sighed. "Not to mention that there are a lot of vampires who consider it the natural order of things for vampires to prey on humans, who see humans as a kind of... stock animal."

Diego thought of Sharon Allen and the other werewolves who had attacked him, and discomfort crept along his spine. Haley had assured him they would stand trial, but Diego couldn't help wondering how many of the werewolves on the jury felt the same way these vampires did. People could be very good at excusing violence against beings they perceived as different or inferior. Diego just didn't know where he, a human-turned-werewolf, fit on that scale. Probably nowhere good.

He probably wasn't doing himself any favors by taking this little road trip either, since he was supposed to stay under observation in Pine Grove until the trial, but that was a problem for Future Diego. Present Diego had other priorities.

"All right. So, this...archon dude doesn't know we're showing up. We've got to convince him letting a murderer run free is bad for business even if he doesn't give a shit about humans, and we can't let the local werewolves know I exist. Am I missing anything?"

"Hit a jackpot?" Val said, the bright sarcasm in his tone making Diego laugh.

"We might stand a better chance with the jackpot, actually," he said. "But the casinos *are* pretty good for late-night buffets if..." He trailed off, glancing at Val. "Well, I guess that isn't really a selling point for you."

What would a buffet for vampires look like anyway? Blood bags all labeled with their different types? Humans lined up with their necks bared? Hell. They could probably get away with something like that, sell it as a tourist experience or something. Nevada could get real weird sometimes. And most vampire media he'd ever seen had some kind of underground subculture of humans who got off on vampire bites.

"It still might be interesting to go," Val admitted, keeping Diego's imagination from veering too far into wondering whether it actually *would* feel good to be bitten by a vampire during sex, or if that was purely pro-bloodsucker propaganda. Could vampires even *have* sex? Didn't you need circulation to maintain an erection, and wasn't a lack of circulation why they had to drink people's bloo—*Focus, Diego.* "Maybe the Bellagio? *Ocean's Eleven* is one of my favorite movies. Mostly the remake."

"The fountain is pretty," Diego admitted. "That's probably worth seeing."

"I guess you probably know your way around pretty well," Val said, and Diego could just see him shift out of the corner of his eye, adjusting in his seat to look more directly at Diego. "Did you spend a lot of time around the casinos, that area?"

"Sort of. A lot of the good concerts that come to Vegas are on the Strip, and my mom is a staff manager at one of the bigger hotels there." He grinned in memory. "All of us, my cousins and me, got jobs in the industry because everyone knew Isela Sanchez knew her shit, and she wouldn't have recommended us if we were going to embarrass her."

Val's voice was warm and almost wistful. "Did you work at the same hotel as she did?"

"Oh fuck no." Diego laughed. "I worked the front desk at a smaller place, off the Strip, until I moved up to Spokane with my cousin

Carmen. She got me on as the night manager at her hotel, with a raise. Figured I would do that long enough to save up for the car I wanted and then...move back home." His throat almost closed on the last word.

The radar detector on his dash beeped quickly, and Diego let off the gas, cruising down to a slower speed and drifting into a cluster of other drivers, grateful to have something else to focus on. He was lucky; there was a shinier, flashier sports car just ahead, swerving from lane to lane like an asshole, and when the inevitable lights flashed from the side of the highway, they were chasing the yellow Ferrari instead of the champagne Audi.

He kept the speedometer hovering around plausible deniability until the prickling feeling of being too close to a cop faded from the back of his neck, and then he gradually eased back up to a miles-per-hour likely to get them to Vegas before the sun came up and did terrible things to his pointy-toothed friend.

"Was it the BMW?" Val said then, and it took Diego several seconds to catch up with the conversation. "The car that you wanted to buy. Was it the BMW that got totaled in Montana?"

"Oh. Yeah, it was." The loss of the BMW still stung. He'd only had it for about a month. "I used to go racing out in the desert sometimes with some friends. One time my friend Micah had entered himself but then sprained his wrist and couldn't drive. He subbed me in to keep from losing the entrance fee." Diego wet his lips like he could taste the Mojave on his chapped skin. "I drove his M-series. I was obsessed instantly and knew I had to have one."

Fuck. Losing the car he'd worked so hard to save for, even if he'd had to buy it used, was almost worse than losing his humanity. Maybe turning into a wolf once a month or so wouldn't suck so bad if he could still drive that car when he didn't have paws.

"I've felt like that about a few things," Val admitted softly, then laughed. "Most recently, Britney Spears concert tickets that I had to resell because I couldn't figure out how to get down to Vegas safely. Now I'm wishing I'd kept them. But security measures have changed since July of 1987."

He knew it was bait, but he took it anyway. Val liked to tell stories about his life, and honestly, Diego liked to listen to them. "You said you were turned in '83, right? What happened in 1987?"

Val sighed, a long, dramatic sound. "Madonna's *Who's That Girl* tour. Her debut! I followed her from Seattle down through Mountain View. I could mostly travel at night, and my ID wasn't expired yet. Barely. And anyway, none of the security guards were looking too closely at my driver's license, since I showed up to every concert in head to toe black leather."

"In July?" Diego laughed.

"Listen, leather was *in* that summer," Val grinned. "And I looked good in it."

Diego shook his head, delighted. "You are so fucking gay."

"Oh, as an Easter parade." Val's smile was audible in the soft nostalgia of his voice, and Diego couldn't help but wonder. If his own pre-werewolf life in Vegas felt like a million years ago, what was it like for Val, who had now been a creature of the night almost twice as long as he'd been a human?

It was a thought that stayed with him as Idaho faded in his rearview, as the lights of Salt Lake City streaked by in the night, across the state line into Nevada, and until the sky began slowly fading from black to blue as he eased the Audi into an empty parking spot in front of the Blooming Sagebrush Motel and cut the engine.

Val was noticeably antsy, fidgeting with his seatbelt as he glanced nervously toward the sky.

"I shouldn't be long," Diego assured him as he climbed out of the car. He was familiar enough with the motel by reputation. It was a few blocks over from the hotel where he'd used to work, and it had never seemed to attract too many sirens of any kind—police, ambulance, fire department. It also had a low nightly rate, which was appealing, even if Val was footing the bill.

The employee behind the check-in desk looked like he was going to have to chug a five-hour energy shot just to get home at the end of his shift. He was slumped over a physics textbook, with glassy eyes that probably hadn't read a single page in hours.

"How long?" he asked Diego without any sort of greeting. "If you're staying past three PM, you gotta pay for two days."

Fair enough; they had to have time to turn over the room for the next guests. Although, judging from the parking lot, the Blooming Sagebrush wouldn't be lighting up the "No" in its "No Vacancy" sign any time soon.

"Three days should be fine," Diego said, just to cover his bases. That should give them enough time to see the archon overnight and sleep through the day afterward. Then they'd be long gone by the time the sun came up on Day Four, and Diego would be in Montana well in advance of the full moon. With any luck, nobody would even realize he was gone.

CHAPTER THREE

"Got some mail, Sommers," Donaldson said into a mug of coffee as Leland walked into the Upham County Sheriff's Office. "Maude's got it at the front desk."

Leland changed course from where he'd been about to settle in for his monthly paperwork duties, heading toward the reception area instead where Maude's desk was. "Sounds fine," he said to Donaldson as he passed the other man with a hearty clap on his shoulder that jostled his coffee precariously. "Gives you time to clean your locker off my desk. Anything still there when I get back is going in the trash."

Being the sole posted law enforcement officer for the little town of Pine Grove meant that Leland didn't spend a lot of time in Red Horse River at the county office, so his coworkers—a generous description—had a tendency to leave their crap on his desk. Fast food wrappers, empty coffee cups, sure, but also the occasional personal item. The door to the hallway closed behind him just as Donaldson yelled, "Walker! Come get your shit!"

Maude looked up over the rim of her glasses when Leland walked into the lobby, but her expression softened into a smile and she put her embroidery to the side.

"Didn't realize we were that close to the end of the month," she said cheerfully. "My favorite day, when you come in and those boys all fall over themselves trying to act like they don't care what you think of them."

"They don't, far as I can tell," Leland said.

"You just think that because you don't care what they think of you," Maude chuckled. "Here, I expect you're here for your mail though."

Leland figured it must be paystubs or something about his insurance —new cards, maybe, and he'd need to mail one to Prudence—but when Maude handed him the envelopes, his vision went dark around the edges and the whole room went a little woozy. The Tucson Police Department crest raised the hairs on the back of his neck, and he tucked the envelope away before he could embarrass himself.

"Now," Maude was saying, picking up where she'd left off with her embroidery, "don't let the sheriff get too close to you today. He's got some godforsaken head cold, and we tried to make him go home, but his wife said he was too much of an ass and sent him back to us. We've got him locked in his office, so take a can of Lysol if you have to go in there."

Leland snorted. "I'll take it under advisement," he said. "Thanks, Maude."

He didn't open the envelope until he'd finished his monthly reports, including the requisition forms for Haley's Halloween plans—parking permits for one of the fields, requests for a deputy to be stationed on the county road that ran along the backside of the preserve to keep tourists from trying to sneak in, traffic management, etc. They'd filled them out together a few nights ago, and he was torn between hoping for a good turnout for her sake and a calm night for his own.

He went into Rylan's office long enough to drop the forms off on the man's desk. "Halloween for Pine Grove," he said, hoping that was enough explanation. It seemed to be; Rylan just nodded and waved him off.

"I'll get 'em processed," the sheriff said in a voice that sounded like he'd stirred gravel into his coffee. Leland nodded his thanks as he left, but his mind was on that thick envelope with the TPD logo on it, and he'd barely gotten into the truck before he had to know what was in it.

He left the keys in the ignition without turning the engine on as he popped open the seal and pulled out the paperwork inside. He skimmed the few short sentences, then read them again when they didn't make sense. *This letter is to notify you that the case you opened against Tucson Police Officer Jacob Niles has been closed. We have determined that Officer Niles's successful completion of canine handling retraining is sufficient to answer the complaint.*

"Son of a—!" He slammed one fist on the steering wheel, the other crumpling the paper furiously. Hell, he had half a mind to drive out to Maddie Shaw's ranch and ask if he could muck her barn just to stuff the contents in this envelope and return it to sender. "Sufficient answer, my ass," he muttered.

He tossed the mutilated letter onto the passenger seat and grumbled to himself as he started the vehicle and turned back toward Pine Grove. It was only the persistent thought of his little sister that kept him driving safely when all he wanted was to floor the accelerator and get some of the rage out of his system. But she was on his health insurance, and it was his paychecks that kept the lights on in their parents' old doublewide, so he needed to keep this job, and wrecking the county's truck wasn't the way to do it.

By the time he'd parked by the curb in front of the tiny storefront that served as the Pine Grove dedicated deputy's office, he'd managed to calm down enough that he figured he'd give his old partner a call, see if she knew anything about it. *Later.* She was probably still on shift, and he didn't want to put her in an awkward position. *Remember that time I tried to turn our coworker in for excessive force and landed in the emergency room and therapy, and then quit my job? Yeah, about that.*

His phone buzzed, and he focused on the screen just in time to see Haley's picture pop up—one of the cutest pictures he'd taken of her over the summer, squinting into the sun, freckled nose scrunched up beneath a peeling sunburn. He'd taken it after a late lunch at a steakhouse in Helena, walking through a park that had a riot of wildflowers growing around a lake with honest to God swans in it.

He'd been taking pictures of the park to send to Pru, and he'd thought about sending the picture of Haley too, but it felt like tempting fate to officially tell his little sister that he was dating someone. Instead, he'd just made it Haley's contact photo in his phone later that evening, while Haley had been passed out on his shoulder.

The text popup faded off his phone screen while he was still thinking about that night, and he rolled his eyes at himself as he opened up the message to actually read it.

Diego finally texted me back at 3am. He's fine. This must be cosmic payback for my teen years. Speaking of, Mom said she'll be here tomorrow. Want to come watch me panic-clean and then we can get dinner?

He snorted softly. He'd witnessed the tail end of more than one panic-cleaning session, which usually consisted of Haley gathering up armfuls of laundry and junk mail out of the living room and dumping them in the second bedroom, then closing the door. He had a feeling that wasn't going to work this time.

Sure, he texted back. *Need me to bring anything? Coffee?*

It was past noon, but chances were Haley hadn't actually been awake that long, and anyway, he'd never known her to say no to coffee. He thought about trading the county truck out for his own Chevy Blazer, but that seemed like a lot of effort, so he just started the vehicle again and turned toward Luann's Diner without even waiting for Haley's answer. He had a feeling he knew what it would be.

For being lunchtime, the diner wasn't very crowded. There were a few couples he didn't recognize, and one man by himself who was inexplicably having a very loud business call on his cellphone at a table by the window.

"No, I said we ought to— Can you hear me? Bob? Bob, you're breaking up. I said—"

"Think I ought to offer him the landline?" Sally Newcrow, co-owner of the diner, laughed as she came up to the counter to greet Leland. "What can I getcha, hon? Coffee?"

"To go, please," Leland confirmed as he pulled out his wallet. "And one for Haley. Not much of a lunch rush today, huh?"

"Nah, kids are in school, and we're off the beaten path for tourists. Most of the Yellowstone crowd ends up in Bozeman or Billings. Got a few leaf peepers driving through." She set a large cup of black coffee down in front of him and popped the lid on, then he watched her pour milk and what seemed like half a shaker of sugar into another cup for Haley. "It's fine though. Gives us a chance to prep for Halloween. This weekend, you won't be able to get through the front door."

"That good, huh? Well, don't go breaking any fire marshal codes." He held out a ten-dollar bill, and Sally waved him off.

"It's on the house."

He frowned and placed the money on the counter anyway. "Tip, then." He picked up both cups and headed toward the door. "See you later, Sally."

She laughed. "Yep. See you and Haley for dinner."

He couldn't even argue with that. It was either the diner or Benny's pizza, because neither he nor Haley could cook worth a damn.

A sharp breeze was blowing in some low-hanging gray clouds as he left the diner, and he wasn't surprised at all when the sky started spitting out little flurries of snowflakes about the time he pulled into Haley's yard. He had to ring the doorbell with his elbow to keep from spilling either cup of coffee, and he started laughing when he could hear the frantic slap of footsteps as Haley ran to the door.

She yanked it open and huffed a frustrated breath when she saw Leland standing there.

"You almost gave me a heart attack, ringing the doorbell," she snapped, swinging the door wide to let him in. "I thought Mom had gotten here early or something."

"Does your mother usually ring the doorbell?" he asked, offering her the cup that Sally had thoughtfully marked with an H, and Haley took it like she was accepting an apology.

"Well, I don't know," Haley complained. "She hasn't actually been back since she moved to Ohio, and she asked me if she needed to complete the pack-visit paperwork, so I don't know how formal she thinks any of this is!"

Leland took a moment to observe her—ponytail starting to slip down around her face, her favorite comfy Seattle Pride bisexual flag shirt smudged with dust, and a wild flush to her cheeks, her brown eyes wide. She was definitely hitting the panic stage.

"You want some help?" Leland looked around the living room, but everything seemed normal enough, not especially messy. "What can I do?"

"You can come talk to me while I'm cleaning out the guest bathroom," Haley said as she headed toward the back of the house, apparently trusting him to follow. "It's boring as heck, so I need a distraction that isn't my brain playing out various scenarios of my mother pointing out every shortcoming I have as an adult and a pack alpha."

Leland hummed into his coffee as he followed her down the hallway. "Well, from what I can tell, that's a pretty short list."

She snorted, tossing a smile over her shoulder. "There you go sweet talkin' me again. But she does this...*thing* where she'll ask me what I'm doing and then say, 'Well, you're an adult, you can make your own decisions,' but what she really means is, 'I think you're making a mistake, but I'm gonna let you find out the hard way.'"

Haley picked up a sudsy bucket off the bathroom floor and pulled out a scrub brush, attacking the shower tiles as she continued.

"Like when I told her I was going to Seattle for college, she just went, 'That's an interesting choice. Are you sure?' Like I was supposed to think it over and realize some piece of information I hadn't taken into account but *she* had, you know?"

"Did you dislike being in Seattle for college?" Leland asked, and Haley huffed, her bangs puffing with the breath.

"No. I enjoyed it. I liked the pack there, liked the city. Balraj was a wonderful alpha, and I learned a lot from him."

Leland gestured with one hand. "Then you didn't make the wrong decision."

Haley dropped the brush back into the bucket with a sigh, soapy water sloshing out, speckling her sweatpants. "I just...I don't know. I want her to be impressed with how well I'm doing, not show up and see the places in the house that still need cleaning, or find something I should've done better with the pack..."

"Well, for what it's worth, *I'm* impressed with you." At her baleful look, Leland opened his arms and chuckled when she shuffled forward into him, dropping her head pathetically against his chest. "You're trying hard, and you very clearly have your pack's best interests at heart. Honestly, what more could anyone ask?"

"Thank you," she muttered, her voice muffled by his shirt as he rubbed her back soothingly. He was suddenly grateful that the Upham County Sheriff's Office didn't care if he just wore a flannel and jeans to turn in his paperwork, because the deputy uniform shirt would not have been comfortable in this position, for either of them.

"Listen, it just started snowing." He pressed a kiss to the top of her head. "Why don't we go drink our coffee out on the back porch and watch it for a little while? And then once you've caught your breath, we'll come back in and take care of whatever you've got left."

She took a deep breath and let it out in a long, soft sigh, then tilted her head back to look up at him. "You have the best dang ideas."

CHAPTER FOUR

THE BLOOMING SAGEBRUSH'S CURTAINS WERE SHIT. THEY WERE SO shit, in fact, that Diego had sacrificed the blankets off one of the beds—*"I guess that one's yours now,"* Val had joked—to try to pin to the curtain rod and block out the sunlight. The thin metal rod hadn't held for more than thirty minutes before it had crashed to the floor, scaring them both awake and flooding the room with early morning light. So, now Val was hiding in the bathroom while Diego got dressed to go buy a new curtain rod and some less shit curtains.

"I don't like you going by yourself," Val complained through the bathroom door, and Diego snorted softly as he picked up the car keys and tucked his wallet into his back pocket.

"Do you not like it worse than sleeping in the bathtub?" Diego tossed back. The sky outside the naked window was lightening to a golden desert dawn that made his throat close with homesickness. "Because those are your two options."

"It's one day. I can sleep in the bathtub."

"Well, I need sleep too," Diego reasoned. "And we can't *both* fit in the bathtub." They could, though, if they squished close together, limbs around each other, his nose tucked into the curve of Val's neck where he *insisted* that he didn't wear cologne—which was such a fucking lie. Diego knew Jean Paul Gaultier when he smelled it.

"At least let me pay for it," Val tried, and Diego rolled his eyes.

"Keep your money, sugar daddy," he scoffed. "I'll be back in an hour or so."

The Audi needed gas—he'd been pushing it to get to the motel before the sun came up—so he stopped there first and then, even though it was farther out of his way than made sense, turned toward Spring Valley before he could talk himself out of it.

The Strip was a glittering rainbow in the distance of his rearview mirror, but the rising sun obscured it with an all-consuming orange fire. The farther he got from I-15, angling south and west from the beacon of the MGM Grand spotlights, the harder his heart pounded, palms sweaty on the steering wheel.

There was a big shopping center out there, he told himself to justify it, but instead of going that way, he took turns he knew by heart into the subdivision where he lived.

Used to live.

By the time he eased the car to a stop across the street from the familiar address, he could barely breathe. His mother's car wasn't in the driveway; most likely, she'd already gone to work. Management shifts started early. But through the living room window, he could see the entertainment center, the same couch that had been there when he'd left two years ago, and a shuffling shadow that could only be his father.

Guillermo Sanchez was a quiet anchor of a man who, for all twenty years of Diego's life, had gotten up before dawn to see his wife off to work. He'd go to his own job later in the day, Diego knew, unless his back was bothering him worse than normal. Isela had been on him to retire early for the sake of his health last time Diego had been home, but the chances of her winning that argument were slim.

Diego had the car door open before he thought about it, one foot out on the curb—and then stopped. He wanted more than anything to go to the front door, to have his father let him in and scold him—*"Where have you been? Your mamá and I have been so worried"*—but the world he lived in now wasn't safe for his family.

No, better to let them go on wondering, for now. Maybe after the tribunal, Haley had said, she could petition the Las Vegas pack to let him join, and he could move back home if he thought it would be safe to tell them. Or if he wanted to spend the rest of his life trying to hide it from them. He didn't have the same concern Haley had felt with Leland—he knew his parents would love him no matter what—but there were so many other pieces to consider. So many other ways it might put them in danger. *Maybe later.* Maybe once he knew better how to protect them.

He took a deep breath and started the car again—and saw the moment that Guillermo heard the engine turn over. He glanced toward the window, idly curious, and Diego held his breath as his father looked straight at the Audi. But maybe he was too far away, or the sun was glaring too brightly, because Guillermo just shuffled off to the kitchen without so much as a second glance.

He was glad he knew the neighborhood like the back of his hand, because between the rising sun and the stinging in his eyes, he couldn't have read a street sign if his life depended on it.

By the time he'd acquired a new curtain rod and some blackout curtains—and fuck, maybe he should've let Val pay for them; why the hell were they so expensive?—he'd mostly managed to put a lid on his feelings. They were here for two days at most. If things went well, he could be back in Pine Grove before Haley got suspicious about his cover story of the vampires letting him stay in Ashton for a little while. He would go back to his new normal, and it was better if he left his old one here.

When he got back to the motel, the bathroom door was still closed. He figured Val had probably gone to sleep; the sun was well and truly up by now. He pulled the rickety chair over and climbed up on it to reach the top of the window, swearing when it wobbled beneath him. He was halfway through wrestling the new rod into place when he heard the bathroom door pop open softly behind him.

"Welcome back."

"I'm not sure you should have that door open," Diego grunted. "Doesn't seem safe."

"I'm fine." A few moments of silence and then, surprised, "You seem to know what you're doing."

Diego let out a strained laugh. "What, did you think I'm too gay to know how to install my own curtains?"

That got a snort out of Val, as he'd thought it would. "No. But you definitely don't seem *butch* enough to know how to install your own curtains."

"Oh, fuck off." He grinned as Val laughed, and then he opened the plastic pack to pull the curtain panels out. They were creased. Oh well. Wrinkled curtains wouldn't be the end of him, even if they did remind him of Carmen's mediocre boyfriend somehow.

"Did you at least pick nice ones?"

Diego gave him his best scathing glance, which wasn't easy considering their relative positions. He got the impression it didn't have much effect. "I picked the only blackout ones in the store. I wasn't exactly trying to match the décor."

"Mm." Val's hum sounded vaguely disapproving, but Diego had other problems to worry about—like getting the heavy-ass panels onto the rod without them slipping off the other end. Maybe Val had a point about him not being able to install curtains. Maybe he should've done this part before he climbed up onto the chair.

He heard the bathroom door open farther, just a whisper across the floor, and held up one hand—a choice he regretted instantly as he had to grab at the curtains again to keep from losing all his hard work.

"Nope," he said sternly to Val, the same way he'd talked to his little cousins when he was babysitting. "Keep that door closed. It's too bright out here."

"You're going to fall," Val muttered. "It's not like I'll burst into flames."

"No, but you'll get very, *very* sick, and I'm not going to talk to this archon fucker by myself."

There, *finally*. With the rod settled in its hardware, the curtains reached all the way to the floor and overlapped each other by a good inch. The room was instantly pitch dark, and Diego had to blink rapidly to try to make his eyes adjust. For just a second, he missed his wolf eyes.

They had much better night vision, and he needed to see how to get off this wobbly-ass chair.

But then he smelled that unique blend of subtle, expensive cologne and dry earth, and one cool hand rested on the small of his back while another one wrapped around his palm and guided him gently down. He hadn't even heard Val come out of the bathroom.

"Thanks for getting the curtains," Val said quietly, just beside his ear, and Diego swallowed hard.

"Thanks for...helping me down."

His eyes were starting to adjust now, and he could see Val as more than a vague shape in the darkness. His soft, white shirt was unbuttoned halfway down his chest, and Diego stared at his collarbones and the dark hair scattered across his pale brown chest as he listened closely. Val didn't have a heartbeat, but Diego could still hear the quiet, slow movement of blood through his body. His own pulse felt quick and fluttery by comparison. Val had the kind of Mediterranean complexion that would probably be a rich, warm, golden brown if he got to spend any kind of time in the sun, but even several decades in darkness and two panels of blackout curtains couldn't completely drain the attractive color from his skin.

"We'll need to get to Hellebore just after nightfall, if we can," Val said, and Diego snapped his gaze up to Val's eyes, fighting the natural instinct to blush. Fuck, what was he, a fifteen-year-old with his first crush? "I looked it up, and we should be safe to leave the motel around six-fifteen tonight."

Right. *Right.* Focus. "Hellebore? What's that?"

"It's the nightclub Jason and his sister own and operate. It's where he hears petitioners."

It took Diego a second to catch up, filling in the blanks, and he scoffed. "*Jason?* The archon's name is Jason? I thought you said he was ancient even by vampire standards."

Val laughed. "He's from Greece. You know, like Jason and the Argonauts. I'm sure it was probably pronounced differently at some point in the past thousand or so years."

Diego hesitated. "But he's not *that* Jason, right?"

Val shrugged. "It depends on what day you ask him, and what he wants you to believe, from what I've heard. But those could all be rumors. I haven't met him."

"He sounds charming," Diego muttered, finally moving out of Val's space. He sounded fucking pretentious and annoying, and Diego's confidence that he was going to be useful at all was steadily dropping.

Val nodded, yawning, his fangs gleaming in the near-total darkness. He covered his mouth with one hand—either to politely cover the yawn or because he saw Diego looking at those sharp canines. They were only slightly longer than normal teeth in his regular state but were still pointed, like a predator. He'd never seen Val with his fangs fully out. The vampire kept a strict schedule with his feedings to avoid the level of hunger that would draw them down.

"I'll set an alarm," Val said as he turned toward the bed where he'd been sleeping before the flimsy curtain rod had collapsed. He sounded half-asleep already, which made sense considering how late in the morning it was and how long their drive had been.

Diego was exhausted too, but his whole body was buzzing with something hot and restless. He got into his own bed, though, and listened as Val's noises quieted, his breathing dropping off slowly until he only inhaled twice a minute. It was unsettling as hell at first, but eventually the rhythm eased Diego's tension until he closed his eyes.

He didn't notice the moment when he fell asleep, but he sure as hell noticed when he woke up—hopefully several hours later—to Val's hand over his mouth and something scratching at the door.

CHAPTER FIVE

Haley could almost forget about her mother's impending visit and Diego's spontaneous vacation with the vampires when Leland had his arms around her. His broad shoulders and barrel chest were warm and solid, and he was calm and steady in a way that Haley didn't think she'd ever been in her life. She hadn't really ever dated anyone like him before either—she was usually attracted to big, bold personalities. Nikki, with her crystals and cleansing and sex magic; Jessie and his band and their dreams of a record contract and a national tour; hell, even her high school misadventures had been with people whose talent for trouble rivaled hers, if not surpassed it entirely in some cases.

The bedrock-like stability that Leland gave off was a complete novelty, but one she was very rapidly coming to appreciate and even crave. His confidence in her was enough to convince her to believe in herself. In fact, curling up against him while he dozed had her feeing downright optimistic. Halloween was just one night, right? She could manage one night. And her mother could visit without filling out paperwork; she was confident in that decision. The permissions filing was a safeguard against attempted coups or wolves avoiding consequences for their actions by fleeing to another pack. Those reasons didn't apply here.

It was late afternoon, and her mother's old room finally looked like someone could sleep there and not like Haley had just been using it as a storage space for months. After coffee on the porch, Leland had helped her move and carry things, and had even helped her make the bed with freshly washed sheets and a quilt that hadn't been out collecting dust. Then, because watching him precisely fold back the flat sheet had sparked an unexpected hunger in her, she'd promptly dragged him to her own bed, which was nowhere near as neatly made, and climbed on top of him.

Now she gently wriggled out from under one heavy arm and slid less than gracefully to the floor in an attempt to keep from waking him. She landed with a soft thump and a giggle, then righted herself and found Leland's flannel shirt to pull on. It was *also* a novelty to be able to wear a partner's shirt, as she was usually curvier than anyone else she dated. She didn't think she could even get her arms through one of Jessie's band tees, but Leland's flannel was big and soft and warm against the chill that crept along the floorboards.

She only bothered buttoning it halfway—if she was really lucky, she might not be wearing it *that* long—as she padded into the kitchen. A glass of water, a handful of pre-Halloween candy, and a piece of cold leftover pizza out of the box in the fridge went a long way toward calming her ravenous, moon-stoked appetite, and she popped a handful of M&Ms into her mouth as she headed toward the dining room table. Or, as it had been ever since she was a kid, the catch-all surface where half-finished projects went to be forgotten, including most of the mail.

Right now, it also held the pack permission papers that she'd pulled out of the filing drawer. She hadn't gotten past writing her mother's name on one of them before getting tangled up in her second-guessing again. Would Kimberly be offended, would she feel unwelcome, if Haley made her fill out forms like a stranger? Or would she be disappointed if Haley didn't follow proper protocols?

The uncertainty rose again while Haley stared at the blank forms, but she shook her head, folded them haphazardly, and shoved them back into the filing drawer for the next time she had to use them for real.

"All right," she said aloud to the quiet house. "Let's really make an impression and clean off this dining table."

Most of it was junk mail that she'd wanted to go through before relegating it to the trash, just in case she missed a replacement debit card from her bank or something. Jessie used to claim they never sent those, just said they did so you had to go into the bank to tell them it hadn't arrived. *"They want you in the building so they can sell you a personal loan or a mortgage or a new credit card,"* he'd insisted more than once. Haley chuckled at the memory now as she tossed several pre-approved loan letters and one extended car warranty scam into her trash can.

Coupon pages, ads for a new crematorium and a remodeled assisted living community in Helena—seriously, how old did they think she was? —and...wait. The crumpled edges of pink and yellow transfer paper peeked out from under a shoebox full of receipts she needed to go through. She tugged the paper free with a sinking feeling of dread, the front page of the triplicate form hanging on by one edge.

REQUISITION FORM was printed at the top, and her breath caught. Oh no. *Oh no, no, no.* It was the form for traffic control personnel, and at the bottom of the front page was the fine print: *Must be received by Sheriff's Office 7-10 days before event start date.*

Great. Just great. It was six days until Halloween; she'd missed the deadline. Maybe she could drive it up the sheriff's office first thing tomorrow. Maybe tonight. Did they have a drop box? Leland could tell her. Maybe she could convince them to take it a couple of days late. If there was a fee, she'd pay it.

But as she turned to go rouse him from her bed, the doorbell chimed for the second time that day. She stood in the archway of the living room, staring at the door as if she could see right through it to her porch. After a moment of silence, she dropped the requisition form back onto the table and started a slow creep toward the door, listening hard to see if she could tell who was out there.

There was a tentative knock and then a very familiar voice: "Haley?"

Oh crap! Why did the universe have it out for her? She swallowed hard as she opened the door, a sudden gust of chilly wind reminding her she was wearing Leland's flannel—and nothing else. *Double crap.* She should've changed before answering the door.

"M-Mom!" she stammered at the tall, blonde woman standing on her porch. "I wasn't expecting you until tomorrow!"

Kimberly Fern gave a nervous, tired kind of laugh and pushed her sunglasses back into her hair. "My flight was overbooked, so they offered me an upgrade if I went with an earlier flight. Then, since it was earlier in the day, I figured I'd just drive straight through instead of getting a hotel. But..."

She glanced out toward the yard, and Haley followed her sightline—straight to the Upham County Sheriff's pickup truck parked there.

"Is the...is everything okay? Or..." She looked back at Haley with a raised eyebrow, and Haley could just imagine what she saw: mussed hair, bare legs, oversize flannel. "Do you need me to go to Luann's and come back later?"

"Oh, uh—"

Haley whirled at the voice behind her, though not before she saw the way her mother's eyebrows went up. And yep, there was Leland, standing in the archway—shirtless, because she was wearing his shirt. At least he had on his jeans and not just his boxers, which under any other circumstances would've been disappointing but right now was an absolute relief.

"Excuse me," Leland said, already backing out of the doorway, gesturing over his shoulder with his thumb. "I'll just..."

"Um," Haley said—eloquently—looking back at her mother. "Maybe just...give me a minute?"

Kimberly laughed gently. "Why don't you meet me at the diner? I'm starving anyway, and we can start over."

Haley nodded. "All right," she said. "We'll...I'll meet you there in a few minutes."

Kimberly looked like she might say something else, but just smiled instead and put her sunglasses back on. "See you in a bit."

Haley watched her return to her rental car, despite the October chill working its way up under Leland's warm shirt, and only closed the door once she heard the engine start.

Haley very suddenly and very deeply wished that swearing didn't still feel so awkward to her. *Thanks for that too, Mom.* Heck, maybe she'd get Diego to help her practice, in case anything like this ever happened again. A couple of well-placed F-bombs sounded great right about now.

She knew Leland was there before he cleared his throat, but the fact that he announced his presence so softly warmed a little place inside her that had gone ice cold over the past few minutes. So many failures, back-to-back, but when she turned to look at him, he had nothing on his face except concern. No judgment, no disdain, and not the bone-deep disappointment she felt in herself.

"Hey, uh, sorry about that," he said gently, rubbing the back of his neck. "I didn't mean to..."

"Well, it's not how I planned to introduce you to my mother," Haley admitted with a wry smile. "But if you want to come to the diner with me for dinner and meet her properly, you're welcome to. I'll even give you your shirt back."

A crooked smile tugged up one side of his mouth. "But you look so good in it." He closed the distance between them enough to tug at the hem. "Barely covers that cute butt of yours."

"Oh God," Haley laughed, hiding her face in his shoulder. "I'm glad she didn't have her new boyfriend with her."

"If you need some time to catch up," Leland offered seriously, "I don't mind. I can fend for myself."

"What, sit across the diner at your own table?" Haley teased. "Or go home and microwave a frozen dinner?" She shook her head. "No, I don't mind. I mean..."

Despite the heat of his bare chest under her hands, a frosty surge of anxiety feathered across her skin. What if she was being too pushy? What if meeting her mother felt too formal, too *committed*, and he felt trapped? She hadn't thought of it like that, but she could see how it carried that weight.

"I mean, if you...if you don't want to, I understand."

He hesitated, and her stomach dropped. Oh God. She *was* pushing too hard. Most people she'd dated had already known her mother—

hazards of a small town dating scene—so this was uncharted territory, and in true Haley fashion, she had miscalculated.

"You haven't seen your mom in over a year, right?" he said gently. "I just don't want to intrude. We can plan to meet up tomorrow, if you want."

"Oh...okay." She didn't know what else to tell him. That sounded like a pretty clear boundary. "Let me...I'll go change, and you can have your shirt back."

She fled the living room before she could embarrass herself any further. She'd done enough of that for one day.

CHAPTER SIX

DIEGO'S HEART POUNDED UP INTO HIS THROAT AS THE SCRATCHING AT the door crescendoed, punctuated by thumps and a hard rattle of the handle. Had the Vegas werewolves learned he was here without permission? Were they going to kill him? What would happen to Val? Did they track him to his parents' house—had he put his family in danger after all?

But then his sensitive hearing picked up the slurring, muffled voices —"...s'not our room, baby, c'mon. We're down here, just one more door..."—and he let out a tense breath.

"What time is it?" he rasped when Val finally moved his hand from Diego's mouth. When Val didn't answer, Diego sat up, squinting at him in the near-total darkness. "You okay?"

"...Yeah." Val cleared his throat and shifted away from Diego, kneeling beside the other bed to open the cooler where he was keeping his juice boxes full of blood. Blood boxes. "Sorry, I didn't mean to—I didn't know if it was safe. I shouldn't have..." He waved one hand, barely visible. "Anyway. I'm sorry."

Diego scrubbed his hands over his face, trying to rid himself of the last vestiges of sleep and Val's touch, then reached over to turn on the bedside lamp. Just past five-thirty PM—their neighbors were getting an early start on their drinking, apparently. But then again, Vegas was a twenty-four-hour city and didn't give a shit about things like nine-to-five schedules.

"It's all right. I should get up anyway and get dressed. How long does it take to get to the...Hellebore club?"

"I'm not sure," Val admitted. "I think we have to walk, at least part of the way. I'm...in the process of getting the details now."

As he said it his phone buzzed, and Diego raised one eyebrow, biting back a sharp comment about how they were cutting it kind of close to just now be nailing down the details. But whatever, Val was the one with the most on the line here.

"I assume dress code is just standard nightclub fare? I didn't bring anything particularly fancy. No leather harnesses or anything like that."

"Couldn't get the pack to lend you a collar?" Val joked lightly, distracted by whatever message was on his phone. The teasing wasn't new, but the surge of rage in response was. Diego swallowed it like sour thorns, but his silence drew Val's attention. "You okay?"

"Yeah." He dropped his duffel bag on the bed and started digging through the clothes he'd brought. Did he have anything nice enough for nightclub fare? The navy guayabera shirt with the blue birds of paradise would show off his arms if he cuffed the sleeves. Leaving it partially unbuttoned would give it more of an evening look, not so much like his dad on vacation. Tucked into the dark slacks, maybe with a belt. He wished he'd brought literally any jewelry; that delicate silver chain he'd left in Spokane would've gone well with this outfit. His earring was going to have to do.

He laid it all out on the bed and stripped his T-shirt over his head, pausing when he noticed Val staring at him.

"What?"

Val narrowed his eyes. "...Nothing." He stabbed a straw into his blood box and sat on his own bed, phone in his lap buzzing occasionally as he ignored Diego.

Diego waited until he was sure Val wasn't looking to roll his eyes. *Fine. Whatever. God, what a drama queen.* He knew he wasn't being reasonable, but *fucking hell.* At least this trip was going to be over soon.

Hell, at this point he was almost looking forward to the full moon. Sure, he'd be a werewolf on his birthday and that fucking *sucked*, but at least as a werewolf he didn't have to think about shit.

"Got it," Val said just as Diego buckled his belt. "Got the exact location and the password."

Diego frowned as he finger-combed his hair into place. *Password?* He shouldn't be surprised; he only knew one colony of vampires, but out of the whole bunch, Val was the least theatrical, and that was saying something.

"It's underground. The entrance isn't too far from here, I don't think." Val turned his phone around so Diego could see the map he had pulled up, leaning in and squinting.

"Yeah. I know about where that is. But you're not gonna want to walk, not from here." He pinched the map, zooming out to get a better idea of the surroundings. "We can probably get away with just walking a couple of blocks, if we park here—"

He pointed to a spot on the map, but a notification popped up just as he did, and when he touched the screen, it opened a message. He stepped back quickly, not wanting to be intrusive, and gestured.

"Sorry, I think you got a text or something, and I just—it opened, sorry."

"Hm?" Val turned the screen back around, frowned, and swiped his finger across the face of the phone to dismiss the text. "Sorry. Where were you saying you wanted to park the car?"

It only took a few minutes to get the logistics worked out, Val marking the route on his phone for reference. While he was waiting for Val to finish getting ready to leave, Diego waited by the door, jingling the car keys in his pocket and trying not to think too much about the text message he had only seen part of.

Happy anniversary, babe!

Who in the hell was sending Val anniversary texts? Was he dating someone? Dating them seriously and long enough to get *anniversary* wishes from them? And why did that idea make Diego want to put his fist through the wall?

"Ready?" Val gestured for Diego to leave first, then followed him out, turning off the lights in the room behind them.

It was easier—sort of—to forget about once Diego was driving them toward the area where Val had indicated on his map, but every time Val's phone pinged, he couldn't help wondering if it was the person who had called Val "babe."

They left the Audi in a parking deck about a block and a half from the non-address Val had been given—an alley between a vape shop and a tourist trap—and Diego tried to keep from looking over his shoulder every five minutes. Some sixth sense prickled at the back of his neck, like they were being followed or watched, but he didn't see anyone. He was probably just nervous about wandering into a den of strange vampires. The ones in Ashton were chill by vampire standards, and even they had to have a formal treaty to keep from wiping out the Pine Grove werewolf pack.

Val paused at the mouth of the alley in question, reading the directions under his breath. "Stairs with a red metal railing that lead down to a solid concrete wall. There's a button under the railing; press it four times precisely. When the enforcer answers the doorbell, tell them the password, and they will take you to the entrance."

"Do I have to say the password too, or will they be satisfied that I'm with you?" Diego asked, tugging his shirt into place and brushing out the wrinkles.

"I think they'll let you in on my word," Val said, but he sounded a little uncertain. There was a very high possibility that Hellebore operated on a vampires-only basis, but they wouldn't know until they got there.

They waited anxiously after Val pressed the button; seconds stretched to what felt like hours, and Diego bit back the impatient urge to ask if Val trusted his source to know what the hell they were talking about.

"You sure this is the right alley?" Diego grumbled after several long minutes, and Val shot him a look.

"Oh, do most alleys in Las Vegas have stairways to nowhere with red metal railings that have buttons under them?"

Diego huffed and rolled his eyes, but it was a fair point. A few more moments, and then— "I think it's me. I think they won't come while I'm here."

"No." Val shook his head. "That's..." He trailed off; Diego had a point too, and they both knew it. He sighed in defeat. "All right, well, now what?"

"I'll go stand out on the sidewalk," Diego said. "And if that's not far enough, I'll go for a walk around the block."

Val's lips pressed together in a thin line, his shoulders drawing in. Tough luck. Diego didn't like it either, but if the enforcer didn't show up to let Val into the club to see the archon, their whole fucking trip was a waste.

After a few minutes, when no one had arrived, Diego signaled to Val that he was going to walk a bit. Maybe not around the block yet, but down to the next intersection and back. And sure enough, by the time he made it back to the mouth of the alley, there was someone speaking to Val—small and slender, a shock of white hair the most visible thing about them in the dimness. Diego held his breath to try to hear better; there had to be *some* good things about being a werewolf.

"...not allowed, not even pets or feeders. You'll have to leave him here," the white-haired vampire was saying.

"He's not a human," Val disagreed. "And he's coming with me."

The declaration that he wasn't human rankled—even if it was technically correct, and even if Val didn't mean it derogatorily. Diego still thought of himself as more human than supernatural creature, no matter what the full moon might have to say about it.

Whatever the two of them said next was lost under a cacophony of car horns and squealing tires from a near miss two intersections away, but then Val turned and gestured for Diego to come down the alley.

Diego followed silently as they were led through an old loading dock to a freight elevator, although he could feel the atmosphere shift as the lift shuttled them underground. The ambient sounds were different, muffled, and he could smell the earth in addition to hydraulic fluid, motor oil, and Val's subtle cologne.

After the lift came a long hallway, and then a door that opened into a massive natural cavern. Amber and crimson lights among the stalactites threw strange shadows onto the smooth floor and across the faces of the people there. Several of them turned as Val and Diego entered, and their guide snorted.

"I warned you. They smell his blood."

Before Diego could protest—either the interest in his blood or being spoken about as if he wasn't present—the guide continued.

"I'll put your name on the register. Someone will be out to speak to you eventually."

"*Eventually*. That's encouraging," Diego muttered under his breath, and Val chuckled softly.

"Well, it can't take too long," he reasoned. "The sun will be up sooner or later."

Diego privately thought that these vamps didn't seem the type to give a shit about whether other people had to be somewhere before the sun was up, since they had this nice cavern to themselves.

He wasn't sure how long they'd been there—an hour? more?—but he was starting to wish he'd thought about the fact that *he* would need to eat when their guide showed back up with a stern companion.

"This way," the guide said. "The archon will hear your case."

Val nodded, but when Diego attempted to follow, a firm hand to the middle of his chest stopped him in his tracks.

"Vampires-only in the archon's chambers," the white-haired guide smirked.

Val looked like he might argue, but Diego was vividly aware that they were massively outnumbered in an unfamiliar, enclosed space. Not the best place to start a fight.

"I'll stay here," he said, meeting Val's gaze. Val frowned, but shut his mouth and followed the guide toward a pair of elaborately carved wooden doors at the far end of the room.

Without Val, though, Diego quickly became a point of interest again. Most were polite enough to just stare at him from afar, but a few inched closer, and one managed to get within arm's reach before he sensed her approaching.

"There's no humans allowed down here," she said in a low, purring voice that thrummed through Diego in places that usually didn't respond to women like that. "But I can hear your heartbeat all the way across the room."

She reached for him slowly, her eyes fixed on his neck, but when he tried to take a step back, he found he couldn't move. Once her fingertips touched his skin, he forgot why he wanted to.

"So, what I want to know," she murmured, green eyes meeting his as she licked her lips, "is what *are* you?"

"**Aimee, stop.**" The new voice, rich with power, snapped through the haze around Diego's mind, and a moment later the hand on his neck was gone. A tall, dark-haired woman pushed the other vampire away, and Diego took a deep, gasping breath as if he'd been underwater for the past few minutes. "This isn't a feeder bar. If you can't behave yourself, I'll throw you out."

Aimee sneered, lip curling to show her fangs, but Diego's rescuer didn't budge, and eventually she slinked away into the shadows, presumably to wait for her own audience with the archon.

The woman who had rescued him left without another word—no small talk, no dire warnings, not even a direct acknowledgment of him—but Diego noticed that everyone in the room gave him a wide berth afterward. In fact, no one even looked at him. He might as well have been invisible. Creepy, but infinitely preferable to feeling like a cracker crumb someone had dropped into a cage full of hungry mice.

When Val reappeared, alone this time, Diego could tell just by looking at his face that it hadn't gone well.

"No luck?" Diego asked quietly. No one was near them, but everyone in the room probably had better hearing than even he did. Val shook his head.

"No. He said that humans aren't his concern, and that any vampire in Las Vegas had the right to feed. Even when I brought up that disappearances mean unwanted human attention and investigations, he just said he didn't have to worry about that. And maybe he doesn't." Val sighed. "But I don't know what else to do. I guess let's...go."

The freight elevator was empty as they rode it back up into the night, and Diego floundered for any way to comfort his friend. But what could he say to ease the sting of knowing that he hadn't been able to stop someone else from being victimized?

As they stepped into the alley, a long shadow fell across their path, and Diego looked up to see the same woman who had rescued him in the club—tall, muscular, with dark hair braided down her back. She stood with her arms crossed, blocking their way.

Ah fuck. The fact that she'd waited to confront them *outside* the cavern could only mean that she didn't want anyone knowing whatever she was about to do to them. The wild thought crossed his mind that Haley was going to be *so pissed off* when she got the news of him being murdered in Las Vegas and found out he'd been lying to her about where he was this whole time.

"My brother is an idiot," she said, and Diego felt Val perk up beside him. "He would destroy everything we've built here for the sake of his arrogance and vanity. You asked for his help finding a vampire who kills, yes? I will help you—but there is a price."

"Oh?" Val glanced at Diego briefly, then back at the woman. She must be the archon's sister, Diego realized. The one who owned and operated Hellebore with him. No wonder her interference had been enough to scare everyone away down in the caverns. "What's your price?"

She looked directly at Diego and smirked, one sharp fang glinting in the reflected neon lights.

"Him."

CHAPTER SEVEN

Leland drove back to his apartment with the persistent feeling that something was wrong. Something *other* than the fact that he'd very nearly flashed Haley's mom and had subsequently chickened out of meeting her face to face at dinner, although that was also definitely a factor.

At least the snow from earlier wasn't sticking and the roads were still clear. Maude had already warned him that during the winter the bulk of his work was going to be rescuing people who'd gotten their vehicles stuck in a blizzard because "it wasn't snowing that bad." A change of pace from Arizona, for sure.

Speaking of which, the crumpled letter from the department was still bouncing around in his passenger's seat. Most likely Guerrera was off work now; he should give her a call. At least that might make him feel like he was *doing* something and hadn't just ditched Haley out of pure chickenshittedness.

Anyway, he should check on her, how she was doing personally. Chances were she had enough sense to stay out of Niles's crosshairs, but she'd been Leland's partner for pretty much the whole time he'd been on the beat, and that might make her a target.

By the time he got back to his apartment, he'd planned what to say.

Just a general checking-up-on-you phone call, no mention of Niles or the results of his complaint. He should check up on Prudence while he was at it, but he knew better than to call her. Depending on their father's mood, a phone conversation might not be the safest idea. Instead, he dashed off a quick text that she could answer when it was convenient and then dialed Guerrera.

Three rings in, he was planning what message to leave on her voicemail, but then she answered, shouting over a ruckus in the background. A party with lots of kids, maybe?

"Sommers! Not that I'm not glad to hear from you, but what the hell are you doing calling me?"

"Can't a guy call his former partner to check up on her without getting the third degree?" he chuckled. Man, for all the shit he'd had to put up with on the Tucson PD, having Mónica Guerrera for a partner had been the best part, and it was good to hear her voice.

"Not when I know you're the kind of guy who doesn't even call a girl back for a second date," she scoffed. He heard what sounded like a door closing, and the sounds of the party faded almost entirely. "You got your letter, I guess. From the department."

"Wh—" He thought about denying it, but there was no point. "Yeah. How'd you guess?"

"I got one too, a couple of days ago. I filed a joint complaint, you know. I didn't see everything that happened that night, but I saw enough, and I figured your story could use corroboration."

"Thanks," he muttered. "For all the good it did. They give you the same song and dance about a canine-handling course?"

"Yeah. Not that I think they even put him through one of those, as pointless as it would be."

Leland sighed, raking a hand through his hair. "I don't know what to do now. There's no appeals process, unless I sue the department, and I'm sure there's no evidence to speak of. It'd be my word against theirs."

"Nothing to be done," Mónica said, and Leland could almost see her shrug. "Move on, friend. Enjoy Montana. Find a girl—or a boy! I don't know your life—and settle down. You did what you can."

What? No. "It's not enough. He's still out there, still on the K9 unit. There's more people he can hurt."

"Sommers, there's always gonna be shitty people in this world, man. You can't get rid of all of them. Sometimes you gotta keep your head down."

"What, so I should've just ignored it and not filed a report?"

"No, I'm not saying that and you know it. I'm just saying you gotta focus on what you *can* change, not waste your energy on what you can't. And sometimes all you can change about a situation is whether or not you're in it."

It wasn't any different than what he'd done so far in his life. Hadn't he left Idaho for exactly that reason? And he'd left Arizona in a similar state of mind. But it didn't sit right to think of Niles still out there on the force, even if he knew the statistics. Even if he knew how many officers kept their jobs—and got promotions—despite record numbers of complaints against them.

His phone beeping interrupted his thoughts, and he cleared his throat. "Well, you take care of yourself," he said quietly. "Niles probably knows we filed the complaints, and I'm sure his personality hasn't improved in the six months since I left."

"I'll be careful," she assured him as the background noises grew louder again; she must have been rejoining the party. "You watch yourself too. I know you're not within easy reach anymore, but he did always have it out for you."

She wasn't wrong. He and Niles had locked horns on more than one occasion. "Let me know if you need anything."

She hung up without a goodbye, which wasn't unusual, and he heaved a sigh. That conversation hadn't exactly gone how he would've liked, but he had to admit she was right that there wasn't much he could do right now. Maybe he'd think of something. Maybe Guerrera would find something that would get the brass's attention. Or maybe Niles would drive his patrol car right off a cliff.

The beep had been Prudence answering his text. He wasn't surprised she hadn't called; this time of day, Earl was probably deep into his beer and Dianne had probably cracked open a bottle of wine. It was only a matter of time from there before Dianne started crying and Earl started yelling, not always in that order. Them overhearing Prudence on the phone talking to their no-good, ungrateful son would just shorten the fuse.

Hey Le :) I'm good. Made a list of colleges, like you said. I only kept the ones with the lowest application fees, but it's still a couple hundred dollars to apply to all of them. Maybe we'll just do it one or two at a time? I've got some savings too.

He frowned, typing back quickly, *Keep your savings and apply to all of them. I'll send you some money.*

A couple of hundred bucks wasn't exactly pocket change, but it wouldn't put him in too much of a bind, and he'd rather Prudence not miss out on a college because she'd waited too late to apply. Maybe once she was finally out of their parents' double-wide, he could get on with his life like Mónica had said and never have to think about Spirit Lake, Idaho, ever again.

Kimberly had gotten to the diner first, which was good, because it meant that Haley didn't have to sit through three quarters of her pack stopping by the table to catch up with their former alpha, only a handful of them. As the last few went back to their own seats, Kim gave Haley an apologetic smile over her cup of decaf.

"Honestly, I didn't think I'd been away long enough for people to act like I was back from the dead," she chuckled, and Haley shrugged.

"People like you. They're just glad to see you." And maybe hoped that Haley's stint as their alpha had just been a temporary placeholder while her mother had been taking a prolonged vacation, she thought privately.

"Showing up at your door also didn't go exactly as planned," Kimberly admitted with a grimace. "I should've called first. I'm sorry. I didn't know you were seeing anyone."

"It's..." Well, it wasn't *new*, was it? Six months was enough time to have told her mother. If she ever talked to her mother about anything substantial. When was the last time she'd brought up her dating life with her mom? "It just hasn't felt like the right time. With everything else going on."

Kimberly nodded, but then cracked a smile. "I have to admit, I'm just glad it wasn't what I thought when I first pulled up and saw the county sheriff truck. You're an adult and can make your own choices, but I really didn't want to know what George was doing at your house."

Haley choked on her water, sputtering. "Mom!"

Kimberly laughed quietly, sipping out of her coffee cup with a smug expression. "Listen, I'm not here to judge..."

Haley shook her head, but it was hard not to smile. This felt familiar and good. It felt like it had before Haley had gone to college, even before high school—back when her mom had felt like her best friend. That had been a long, long time ago.

"Don't take this the wrong way, Mom, but why *are* you here?"

Kimberly laughed, but...was there something underneath it? Or was Haley just making things up? "Nobody does Halloween like Pine Grove," she said. "It's bigger than Christmas. I wouldn't have missed it for anything."

"Your new pack in Ohio doesn't do anything for it?" Haley wondered.

Kimberly shook her head. "Not like this. They were just going to have the regular full moon run. There aren't a lot of places around Columbus that're safe for a pack of wolves. There aren't any wild packs, just a few coyotes here and there, so we have to be cautious."

"I'm surprised Dennis didn't want to come see what it was all about then," Haley mused, increasingly aware that it felt like she was giving her mother the third degree. But once she started asking questions, there were so many others...

"I thought it would be nice if it was just the two of us again." Kimberly smiled. "I didn't really get to see you when you got home from college, what with moving... Although if I'd realized you were seeing someone, I would have made more specific plans. And I might've called earlier."

There. Something *was* wrong. Haley hadn't been certain at first, with all the sounds and smells of the diner, but something was off about Kimberly's pulse and breathing, and there was a subtle scent of anxiety clinging to her. All of Haley's instincts said her mother was, if not lying, at least not telling the whole truth.

Sure, Halloween had been their special time. Kimberly wasn't wrong in saying it was a bigger deal than Christmas. On years when it didn't fall on a full moon, she and Kimberly had taken turns playing guide to tourists while the other led the pack in a rousing, howling run. And on the rare occasions when neither of them could be human, they would split the pack between them and Haley would herd the tour groups toward the edge of the woods, where her mother would let them catch just the barest glimpse of her hulking, shadowy physique in the alpha form—just enough to make them doubt their eyes.

It was better than any haunted maze or escape room she could think of. Kimberly was right—nobody did Halloween like Pine Grove. But that wasn't all there was to it, Haley was certain.

Why are you really here?

CHAPTER EIGHT

Tiffany—because of course an ancient Greek vampire named Jason had a twin sister named Tiffany—had led them away from the entrance to Hellebore, presumably so the archon wouldn't overhear when she said, "My brother is wasting the empire we've built on petty territory disputes and stroking his own ego. I intend to take it from him—and I need your little werewolf to do it."

"What do you need me for?" Diego snapped, grumpy at continually being spoken about as if he was not present and articulate. "I thought vampires and werewolves don't get along."

"Which is where you come in." Tiffany finally turned to look at him, intimidating and imperious. Diego almost wished she would go back to ignoring him. "Jason is attempting to expand his territory across the borders of the local werewolf pack. So far there have only been skirmishes, but it is escalating toward an all-out war. I want to offer them an alliance."

"That's great and all, kudos to you for...reaching across party lines or whatever," Diego said, "but I can't help you with that."

"Get me a meeting with their alpha."

Diego snorted. "Lady, I don't think you understand me. I'm not even supposed to be here. If they catch me in their territory, I'm going to get my ass kicked. You'll want to befriend one of the locals instead. C'mon, Val, let's get things packed to go home."

He'd barely turned when she said, "I know where to find him," and Val froze, nostrils flaring with a sudden intake of breath.

"You do?" Val asked softly, at the same moment Diego challenged, "Who?"

Tiffany smirked. "You came to petition my brother about a vampire, right? David Hale? I know where you can find him—and you won't find him without me. My brother is sheltering him as part of his coven."

Fuck! Diego looked at Val immediately, a chill running down his spine. If the archon was sheltering Val's attacker, that meant the attacker knew they were here. Knew where Val was. Knew Val was attempting to have him brought to justice.

"You know what he's done?" Val challenged in a quiet voice, then frowned when Tiffany shrugged.

"He's a vampire. He's doing what vampires have always done. It's not my business what you want with him. I'm just offering to help you, in exchange for the use of your little pet."

Val opened his mouth, but Diego had had enough.

"God*damn,* I'm tired of you people talking about me like I'm an animal," he growled. "How do we even know you're telling the truth anyway? I might get myself thrown in werewolf jail trying to help you, and then it turns out you don't even know where this Vampire Dave fucker is."

"That is fair," Tiffany said calmly. "As a gesture of goodwill, I will tell you that he tends to favor finding his meals at two of the local feeder bars." She reached into her coat and pulled out two business cards, handing them to Val. Diego peeked over his shoulder but couldn't make out more than the shimmering red text on one of them. "He was not at Hellebore tonight, and there are a few hours left until sunrise. It's possible you could find him." She waved one hand carelessly. "Though I fail to see what action you'll take if you do. He is older, stronger, and he has my brother's protection. However, I wish you good hunting. You may contact me if you wish to broker an agreement."

She turned without waiting for any sort of response, presumably headed back down into the caverns, and for all that it was probably just his imagination, the street did feel lighter, less oppressive, once she was gone.

"Well?" Diego said after a moment of Val staring at the two business cards in his hands. "We could pick one and try it out."

The look Val gave him was almost pitiful, the crease in his forehead and the downturn of his full lips. "She's right," he said hoarsely, shaking his head. "I don't know what I'd do if I found him."

We go groveling to her about it, which is her whole game, Diego almost said, but he wasn't entirely convinced she wasn't still lurking around somewhere she could hear him. "Well, let's cross that bridge when we get to it," he said aloud. "Pick one."

Val handed him one of the cards with a heavy sigh, and Diego felt his eyebrows go up. "The Juice Bar? What the fuck?"

"She said it's a feeder bar," Val said. "That means any humans who go there go on purpose."

"Jesus, what's the other one called? Ye Olde Smoothie Shoppe?"

That at least got a dark smile out of Val. "If you're sure you want to go, we can go. You might be the subject of a lot of unwanted interest though."

"We might as well. Aren't you always telling me werewolves smell bad? Maybe that'll come in handy for once."

"It's not...that bad," Val said weakly as he followed Diego back toward the parking lot where they'd left the Audi.

Val stayed quiet as they buckled in and Diego put the Juice Bar's address into his GPS. Before Diego could put the car in gear, though, he spoke up again.

"I don't...I don't think I want David to know I'm here." He wet his lips, and Diego spotted the way his tongue pressed against one sharp canine tooth afterward, a familiarly anxious gesture. "I didn't realize..."

"Okay." Diego hesitated, trying to stay calm and think through the situation. "I don't know what he looks like, though, to find him. What if we keep you low-profile? I can be the bait. That way he doesn't have to know you're here."

Val's frown deepened. "I don't really like that either."

"It's not like we thought this was going to be a trip to Disneyland, Val," Diego snapped in frustration, then took a deep breath through his nose to try to calm down. "Listen...I appreciate that you want to keep me safe. But we wouldn't be doing this in the first place if it wasn't important. We'll be careful, but if we don't try, then what's the point of any of this? We could have just stayed in Montana."

Val's silence hung in the air between them all the way to the Juice Bar, which—against all odds—was an actual juice and smoothie bar during the day. The sign taped to the door said *After-hours deliveries: Back door, ring bell,* and Diego gestured around the side of the building.

"That's us, I guess." He eyed Val. "Are you gonna be okay with this?"

One of the things Diego had learned from his friendship with Val was that breathing was semi-optional for vampires—their systems were slowed down enough that they only needed to breathe occasionally to maintain oxygen levels—so the long, shaky inhale and soft, sustained exhale was just pure nerves.

"I have to be," Val said quietly. "You're right. If I can't even do this much..."

Diego swallowed hard against the impulse to hug him, squinting into the streetlights instead. "Well, he wasn't at Hellebore tonight, according to Tiffany, so there's no real way for him to know you're in town yet. And it'll be dark in there. This is probably the best chance we've got."

He worried they'd face the same trouble getting into the Juice Bar as they had at Hellebore, but the bouncer waved them through without a second glance. The benefits of being a feeder bar, Diego guessed. They had to let the food in.

After the surreal elegance of Hellebore's caverns, Diego hadn't known what to expect of this one, but it wasn't the neon-and-blacklight 80s dive bar that he walked into. The Juice Bar sported dark-painted walls, prisms hanging from a chandelier that threw trembling rainbows across the floor, glass top tables, and a giant mirror behind the bar. Diego was a little disappointed that the no-reflection thing seemed to be a myth; he could see Val's stormy expression just fine between the bottles of blood and Jack Daniels.

But he wasn't here to watch Val. If he was going to be bait, he needed to get out on the floor and look...well, tasty. It was hard at first to not be on high alert, trying to tell who was a vampire and who wasn't, examining the few faces he could make out in the dim, multicolored lights. What would he do if he saw someone he knew here?

Eventually he managed to push it all to the side and remember how to act at a club. He danced with a few casual partners, none of whom had fangs, but they all seemed more concerned with advertising themselves to other people. More accurately, to vampires. No human here was looking to hook up with another human.

As he started to turn away from his most recent dance partner, the beautiful dark-skinned man he'd been swaying with caught his elbow gently. Diego turned back to him with a *Sorry, I'm not looking for anything serious tonight* on his lips that died instantly at the man's expression.

"I don't know if you're here to cruise, but he—" The man gestured discreetly toward the bar. "—hasn't taken his eyes off you the whole time. I wanted to give you a heads-up, just in case."

"Thanks." Diego swallowed and watched the man dance off with a different partner, then steeled himself to turn and look. Was it Vampire Dave? Was it going to be that easy?

But the only person at the bar who was looking out at the dance floor was someone else entirely. Val sat clutching a tumbler full of dark liquid, unmoving, eyes occasionally reflecting the rainbow lights as he watched Diego like he was going to eat him alive. Diego's pulse jumped, a twist in his stomach like an answering hunger...and then he was suddenly aware of the way the noise level in the club dropped by half.

Several people—vampires, he realized when they bared their teeth—turned sharply toward him, nostrils flaring.

"Hey." Thin arms in fishnet gloves wound around him, turning him away from the bar and toward a very petite girl dressed in clashing patterns of black light reactive neon. "I'm Rayne. What's your name?"

"What?" Spell broken, Diego put his hand on Rayne's arms to try to push her away, but her grip tightened. "Look, I'm sorry but—"

"You need to calm down." She leaned in closer, lowering her voice. "Every vamp in here can hear your heartbeat right now."

He stared down at her and realized her neck was a crisscross of pale and pink scars above a tattoo of a single red blood drop on her collarbone. "Are you human?"

"Yeah." She smiled at him. "You are too, right? First timer?" When he just stared at her, wordless, she shrugged. "I've never seen you around the scene before, and you seem really nervous."

"The scene— So—" He paused, thoughts racing. This was a thing? This was a whole underground *thing* that people in his home city just... knew about and participated in? How widespread was it? He hadn't expected his wild imaginings to actually be *true*, not even when Tiffany mentioned a feeder bar. Rayne's scars, her tattoo, the way everyone seemed to be trying their best to show off their necks and wrists—it all spoke a language he hadn't even known existed but these people seemed fluent in.

"Oh, you're *new* new." She pulled him closer, starting to dance a little, and he went along with it. She wasn't his type, but the good news was that meant his pulse was starting to come back down to normal. "Can I give you some advice? Try not to be *too* eager. You need to stay as calm as you can, unless you're with someone you know really well and trust to have good self-control. Do you know what a blood haze is?"

Diego shook his head. "No, but I can guess from the context."

"Yeah, it's probably what you're thinking. They have no control over what they're doing, and even if they don't mean to hurt you, they can completely drain you. It can happen if they haven't fed recently, or if they're very excited."

Well, that sounded like bullshit. Surely, they had *some* control.

But then he remembered: Lightning. Mud. Blood in his mouth. The fact that he still didn't know if he'd killed a man in the throes of his first transformation.

All right. So maybe vampirism had some complications he didn't know about, and things like "blood hazes" weren't just excuses to indulge their worst impulses. Maybe. It was possible.

"What happens if they drain you?" Diego asked, pitching his voice low when he noticed a sharp glance from one of the vampires sprawled in a velvet chair to the side of the dance floor.

"You die," Rayne said. "Although some of them know how to make fledglings—new vampires—if they drain you, so you might wake up with a new set of fangs."

"I already have too many of those," Diego muttered without thinking, but Rayne just laughed.

"Anyway, if you decide you want to really dip your toes in, there's an older guy who comes in sometimes whose kink is virgins." When Diego opened his mouth to argue, she clarified, "Blood-virgins. Unbitten."

Before Diego could protest that it still didn't apply to him—thanks, asshole fascist werewolves—he realized that it might very well be the vampire he was looking for. "Oh?"

She nodded. "I've never been with him. I'd already been bitten by the time I met him, and he only likes unmarked necks. Never bites the same person twice."

"**Rayne**." A voice from the lounge area thrummed between them, the same unnatural—*super*natural—weight to it that Tiffany's had when she'd rescued Diego from the hungry vampire at Hellebore. "**Come here**."

"Oh, that's my cue." Rayne smiled cheerfully. "I'm here with someone —I just didn't want you getting in over your head." Her smile hardened a bit as she stepped away from Diego. "Not to mention how mad I'd be if *my* vampire got all hot and bothered about *your* pulse tonight, so keep it down."

Message received, then. He watched, just to note who she went to, to make sure he didn't piss off a tiny scene girl with the kind of pain tolerance she clearly had. But it was a woman—a ferocious, terrifying-looking woman, for all that she was probably barely five feet tall—who hauled Rayne into her lap and started stroking her neck. And, that weird moment with Aimee aside, Diego had never experienced sexual attraction to women. He was safe on that front.

Maybe not any other front though.

For the first time, he thought maybe he'd gotten in over his head. Maybe he should've stayed out of this, let Val talk him into packing their bags and checking out of the Blooming Sagebrush to drive home.

This time when he met Val's eyes across the bar, Val gestured with one thumb over his shoulder and a questioning tilt to his head. *Wanna get out of here?*

And the answer was yes. He really, really did.

CHAPTER NINE

LELAND WOKE UP WITH THE MOST GODAWFUL HEADACHE HE COULD ever remember and a tickle in the back of his throat. A rummage through the few boxes in his bathroom didn't come up with any painkillers, so he could only hope a cup of coffee and his best pair of sunglasses would be enough to get him through the morning. He could just kick back in the office and take it easy, at least. Almost no one ever stopped by the deputy liaison's office unless they were just there for a friendly chat.

But today, of course, it was just his luck that the second he was inside and had closed the shades to make it as dark as possible, there was a frantic rap on the door. He opened it to find Haley standing there, clutching a piece of paper, although she snapped her mouth shut on whatever she'd been about to say as soon as she saw him.

"Are you all right?" She gestured to her own face. "You look kinda pale and you're wearing your sunglasses in a dark room."

"I'm fine. Just a little headache. What did you need?"

She frowned but let him redirect her. "I found a form yesterday that I think I left out of the ones you took up to the sheriff's office. I'm going to drive it up today, but it needs your signature before I drop it off."

He stepped back to let her in, gesturing to the desk. "Sure. Which one is it?"

"Traffic control personnel." She smoothed it out on the desk's surface, although it didn't do much to change the creases. The carbon copies were going to be a mess. "It looks like we got partway through filling it out. I finished it this morning, but you have to sign it."

They'd had a paperwork date at Haley's house a week or so ago, where they'd gone through everything together and then celebrated the end of it by getting naked on her living room floor. Maybe they'd been too excited to get to the celebration and hadn't checked everything as carefully as they should have.

Leland took a second to glance over what she'd filled out, although most of the print ran together in a blurry mess, and he had to squint to make the letters come into focus. Whatever, she was a smart woman. He was sure she'd filled it out just fine without his help.

He scribbled his signature beside the date she'd already written in, then reflexively checked to be sure it had gone through all the carbon copies. She reached for it, barely stopping herself from snatching it away from him, her usual eagerness to be in motion, to be doing *something*, shining through.

"Thanks," she said when he handed it to her. "I need to turn this in so I can get back before Mom is up and around. She's sleeping in right now, after the travel yesterday but..." She paused, tilting her head at him. "Are you *sure* you're all right?"

"Hm?" It took a bit of effort to tune back in to actively listening instead of just letting her words wash over him. "Yeah, I'm fine. Just a headache."

"Do you get migraines?"

The question was gentle, but it slammed into Leland like a freight train.

The baby was crying. "Mom, the baby's crying."

"Shh, honey. Mommy has a migraine. Shh." The clatter of a half-empty prescription bottle rolling under the bed as Dianne pulled the blankets up. "Close the door, okay?"

"No," he said, harder than he intended. "I'm fine." He held out his hand for the paper he'd just handed her and said, "I'll take that up to the office."

"It's all right." Haley took a step back from the door. "You were just up there, and it's my fault this didn't go with the others. I'll just ask if I can still turn it in, even though it's a day or so late."

There was no reason for that to bother him as much as it did, but it ground through him like a slipping clutch, and he scowled. "I said I'll take it." When she frowned, he slid his sunglasses off, despite the way it made his headache spike, and consciously softened his voice. "You don't need to worry about this. Spend some time with your mom doing fun stuff. Werewolf stuff. Whatever. This is my job."

"All right," she said, irritatingly slow and suspicious, holding out the form to him again. "Hey, when you get back, do you want to grab lunch? You can meet Mom now that it's not, you know, a weird surprise. What do you think?"

The answer was no, he really didn't, but he didn't have any convenient excuses today that wouldn't cause more trouble than he wanted to deal with. "Uh, yeah. I'll text you when I'm back in town."

The way she visibly relaxed at his answer made him feel like an ass for running out on her the night before.

"Okay." She smiled. "And don't, like, don't worry about it. It's not a meet-the-parents formal kind of thing, I promise. She's chill."

Leland decided it would be uncharitable to point out that Haley had just spent a week panicking about seeing her mom and leaned in to kiss her cheek. "So, no *what are your intentions with my daughter* talk?" he teased, and she snorted.

"No, I'm more likely to get the third degree about it than you are. And anyway, it's not like she has any room to talk." She turned back at the door, eyes bright with what he recognized as a sudden idea. "Oh hey, if you want, we can go to Great Falls, and all be on neutral ground instead of the whole town eavesdropping on us at Luann's."

Well, that was more appealing than he'd strictly expected. "Great Falls could be nice," he admitted. "Why don't you let me know when you start that way. I'll do some work around the office while I'm in Red Horse River and just meet you there."

Haley left in a better mood than she'd arrived in, and Leland figured he'd bought himself a few minutes to take control of things before they went off the rails. All right. So, he'd take the forms up to Red Horse River, and he'd get ibuprofen and a cup of coffee and ask Maude what the hell kind of thing he ought to say to his girlfriend's mom whom he hadn't expected to have to meet yet.

It was a simple enough plan, but he had trouble holding each individual step in his mind. He remembered the ibuprofen but almost left his coffee sitting on the counter by the cash register. Went back to get the coffee, almost drove back to the office in Pine Grove instead of going on to Red Horse River. Parked, locked the county truck, and was halfway to the building before he remembered that he was supposed to be taking the forms in and had to turn around to go get them. *Damn. I need to get more sleep.*

Rylan was still in his office, with the door closed, and Walker and Donaldson made a show of moving far away when Leland opened the door to go in. The whole office smelled like cherry cough drops, with tissues stuffed into the wastebasket beside the desk, and as Leland placed the last rogue form onto the desk, Rylan uncapped a bottle of cough syrup and tilted it back for a long swig.

"Sommers," he wheezed when he recapped the bottle. "Wasn't expecting to see you."

"Left out one of the forms," Leland said, handing it over.

Rylan frowned as he studied it. "You know this is past the deadline."

"And it wouldn't have been if I'd turned it in with the others," Leland argued. "It fell down between the seats and I didn't realize it 'til later. Besides, I'm the one you'll be assigning for traffic control, so it's not a big deal."

"Donaldson and Walker are on traffic control," Rylan said, but he did pull out the rubber stamp, change the date back one day, and stamp *Received* at the bottom. "I was gonna put them on crowd control with you, but the loaners can do that."

"Loaners?"

"Gotta borrow a few from Meagher County. Was gonna put them on traffic, but I can't turn in the form late to *their* office. So. Walker and Donaldson on traffic, you and the loaners on crowd patrol."

Leland barely stopped himself from scoffing. His coworkers would be bad enough, but officers he *didn't* know sounded like a nightmare. "Surely, we don't need that many. There's, like, fifty people tops in that whole town. What, we get a couple dozen more from the area around?"

Rylan gave him a scathing look over a handful of tissue as he blew his nose. "Halloween is on a Saturday night with a full moon this year, in a town that drums up its damn werewolf legend more than Santa Claus, and you think we'll get a *couple dozen* tourists? We'll be damn lucky if Meagher has enough people to send us."

Well, shit. Leland hadn't realized it was that big of a deal. Sure, Haley had mentioned, but he'd honestly thought maybe she was exaggerating a bit. Like Sally had said, Pine Grove was just too far out of the way for tourists.

"Point taken."

Officers from the next county over, huh? Maybe Maude could tell him about them. He realized that while he hadn't taken her too seriously when she'd said Walker and Donaldson wanted to impress him, he did think he could probably throw his weight around with them. Unknowns were a wildcard. There might be someone like Niles mixed in—or worse.

But Maude was out for the day, something about her granddaughter's birthday, and Donaldson was watching a football game on his phone with the volume turned all the way up, so Leland retreated to his truck and decided to take his chances with his cell signal to try to search up any news stories out of Meagher County. He got very little for his efforts, just some public interest filler about county fairs and fundraising, and he had to wonder if it was because nothing had ever happened or because they'd covered it up. Hell, had there even been a story about what had happened to him in Tucson? He was trying to decide whether to look, knowing either result would piss him off, when his phone buzzed in his hand.

I let Mom pick the restaurant. We're leaving in a few minutes, probably be there around 12:30.

Immediately following was the name and address of a steak and seafood place, and any other day that would've sounded great. Today, though, he just wanted to be home and unconscious. His eyes were starting to feel gritty on top of the headache, and he rubbed them with one hand while he texted a reply to Haley with the other.

OK. See you there.

And maybe if he'd been in his own SUV, which had a hands-free mount that fit his cellphone, unlike the county truck, he wouldn't have put the phone on the passenger's seat. And then the phone wouldn't have slid off into the footwell when he had to brake for a family of pheasant in the road, and it wouldn't have gotten wedged under his foot.

And maybe if he'd felt slightly less like shit, none of that would've been enough to make him overcorrect straight into the ditch.

CHAPTER TEN

Diego flopped onto the bed as soon as they got to the motel room. He'd have to get up and change clothes in a minute, but he also might need to go to the office to extend their stay, depending on what Val had in mind.

Val, however, wasn't giving any hints. He stood at the window, the blackout curtains tucked back for the moment, staring out at the neon and streetlights. Diego did his best to give him time, but he hated uncertainty on his best days, and five days from a full moon was far from a best day, with the impending wolf prowling under his skin.

"Well?" he finally prompted when he couldn't stand it any longer. "What do you want to do?" When Val didn't say anything, just sighed, Diego tacked on impatiently, "Are we staying another night or are we going back to Montana?"

"I don't know," Val answered, low and pained. "You agreed to drive me down here for two nights, and this was it. I was prepared to deal with the archon not seeing me or telling me he wouldn't take the case and having to settle for hoping word got out enough that someone would do something. I...wasn't prepared to learn that the archon is actively sheltering him and condoning his behavior."

"Tiffany—" And Christ, what kind of a stupid fucking name. Next thing he knew Val was going to be telling him *Tiffany* was a popular name in ancient Greece too. "Tiffany said he mostly goes to those feeder bars, and you said yourself all the humans who go there are there by choice. So maybe he's found a healthy outlet."

Val snorted. "There's no such thing as a *healthy outlet* for what he did."

All right. Understandable, since Val had implied he hadn't wanted to be turned. Maybe Vampire Dave had gone into one of those blood hazes Rayne mentioned and it had all been a terrible accident. Or maybe he'd been a dick on purpose.

"She also told you she could find him," Diego said. "Say that I *did* get into this for her and find some way to get a message to the Vegas alpha." When Val huffed, Diego held up one hand. "Just—just for argument's sake. Say I did. Say she shows up with Vampire Dave all wrapped up in a bow and hands him over to you. What...what would you do?"

Val's silence spooled out, longer and longer, but this time Diego didn't interrupt. This was a hard question.

When Val finally spoke, though, it wasn't an answer. Not directly, at least. "I never told you exactly what happened, when I was turned," he murmured. "I think you should know."

Diego sat upright on the bed, but Val was still staring out the window.

"All right," Diego said quietly. "I'm listening."

"It started the day I moved out into my own apartment..."

"Welcome to independent adulthood! Let's go out drinking to celebrate." Don whooped, swiveling his hips as he stripped out of his tank top and swung it around over his head. Jim, Don's partner of two years, shuffled him out of the way as he and Val struggled to get the single-width mattress around the corner of the tiny apartment and into the bedroom.

Val didn't have a bed frame yet—or any furniture, actually—but that was all right. The apartment came with a stove and a refrigerator, and Jim and Don had generously gifted him this mattress. The important thing was that he had his own place; making it into the place of his dreams could wait.

"I should finish unpacking and buy groceries, I think," Val said, but Don just snorted.

"Unpacking *what*? Anyway, the grocery store will be there tomorrow. Put on your ruby slippers, Dorothy! The Yellow Brick Road awaits."

Even Jim, who was arguably the more responsible of the pair, was in agreement. "First round's on us," he said. "As a housewarming."

And really, how was Val going to turn that down?

There were a few people he knew at the Yellow Brick Road, and every single one of them offered to buy him a drink as soon as he said it was his first day in his own apartment. Twenty-two years old and out on his own for the first time; his parents were convinced he'd be dead or in jail within forty-eight hours. And, well, it wasn't as likely in San Francisco as in other areas of the country, but the cops did raid Castro bars sometimes too.

He wasn't sure when the man at the bar started watching him, only that Don pointed him out right before he arrived at their table.

"I haven't seen you around before," the man said, ignoring Jim and Don and staring straight at Val. He wasn't exactly handsome, but he was oddly compelling, and Val found it impossible to look away from his face. "I'm told you're celebrating."

"I just moved into a new apartment," Val said, and even he was surprised at the breathless quality to his voice. "Today."

"Well, congratulations then." The man held his hand out to shake. "I'm David. It's nice to meet you."

The moment their palms touched, Val felt completely intoxicated. His gifted cocktail sat unfinished on the table, gathering sweat, as Don and Jim went...somewhere. He didn't even know where. His single-minded focus was on David and the absolute biological necessity of David's attention and approval. By the time Jim came to let him know that he and Don were headed home—with a glance at David to give Val the *If you want an out, we're it, right now* cue—Val had forgotten he'd even arrived with friends. In fact, when Jim first touched his shoulder, Val didn't recognize him.

“I can’t believe I lost track of what time it is,” he laughed, and David reached out, one hand resting lightly on Val’s wrist.

“You don’t have to go yet,” he said, staring straight into Val’s eyes. “I can take you home if you want to stay longer.”

Jim frowned, but Val didn’t even register his expression over the surge of butterflies in his stomach—butterflies that felt like they were pulling him like a chariot directly into David’s arms. “Yeah. I want to stay.”

Val paused, gathering himself, and Diego was back in the motel room, soft lamplight spilling onto the floor between the twin beds. Val had come away from the window and was sitting on the other mattress, hands clasped loosely between his knees as if he didn’t know what else to do with them.

“What happened?” Diego’s voice felt almost rusty from disuse, even though Val couldn’t have been talking for that long. It felt like an eternity.

“He didn’t kidnap me or anything. He didn’t have to. The pheromones and my eagerness to have a partner were enough. I didn’t even realize he was drinking my blood at first. What a weird thing to think, you know? I thought he was just biting, like a sex thing. The bite marks always healed into bruises, so I thought I was just...discovering a kink.”

He sighed, staring up at the ceiling, and leaned back against the pillows and the headboard.

“My friends saw the problem first. I was getting paler. I was sick all the time. I didn’t want to go out with them. I stopped going to work. The only thing I talked about or thought about or *wanted* to think about...was David. After a few months, Jim and Don and a couple of other friends from the community center came to my apartment and wouldn’t let me leave until we’d talked.

“They brought me food. I hadn’t managed to buy any since I moved in. I hadn’t even *wanted* any unless David suggested it. But they brought food and made me eat, and when my head was clearer, they told me I had to break up with David for my own good. I didn't want to hear it, not even when they pointed out all the red flags."

The twist of Val's lips was so bitter that Diego could taste the regret on his own tongue, sour and guilty.

"I accused them of lying, of exaggerating, but Jim had taken pictures and developed them in his own dark room. The bruises I didn't remember. The bite marks that had been there before they healed over. I remember in one of the photographs, my eyes looked so...empty."

He turned on his side to face Diego, sorrow in his expression.

"It took them almost a whole day to convince me he wasn't good for me. I think they thought he was drugging me. The bites on my arms could've been track marks. None of us knew, you know? Vampires weren't real. So, I called David and asked him to meet me at the club where we'd met. Jim suggested doing it in public, in case things turned ugly. He and Don promised to come with me."

"Did it?" Diego asked softly. "Turn ugly, I mean."

"I don't know." Val shrugged, and his face looked especially hollow in the shadows cast by the lamp. "I remember waiting for David to get there, Jim and Don sitting a few tables away. The next thing I remember is...waking up in David's basement."

Icy cold dripped down Diego's spine and into the pit of his stomach. Absolutely nothing good could follow those words—and somehow, he knew it was even worse than just being turned into a vampire.

"There's—it's a muddle," Val continued after a long silence. "I'm not sure how long I was there. Hours, days, weeks? I didn't stay conscious very long at a time. I woke up enough to know he was drinking from me regularly, and occasionally he woke me up to make me eat. One day, I realized I wasn't strong enough to escape. He was feeding me just enough to keep me alive, but not enough that I could *do* anything. I was going to be there, chained up in that horrible basement until he bled me dry. So, I...tried to kill myself. I remember passing out, thinking that was it, I was dying. And I guess I did."

Some of them know how to make fledglings, if they drain you, Diego remembered Rayne telling him at the Juice Bar, and he had an awful feeling he knew what came next.

"He must've gotten home pretty soon afterward. From what I understand, it has to be done while the person is still...warm." Val snorted. "I don't know why he turned me. Vampires can't be nourished by each other's blood. Maybe it was out of spite or revenge. But there's this thing that happens when you're turned—it's a flood of pure adrenaline, enough to reanimate your body. I think they call it a *moonrise*. But it was enough that I fought him off. I thought I killed him, but I learned later it takes more than just stabbing to kill a vampire. Beheading or strong, direct sunlight are pretty much your only options."

"So, when he says he's looking for your replacement..." Diego shuddered. "I thought you meant he wanted a vampire to raise as his protégé. But you mean he wants someone to..."

"To lock in his basement and feed on until they die," Val murmured.

What. The. Fuck. What the actual goddamn fuck. For all that Diego sometimes still woke up in a sweat, hearing Sharon Allen shouting after him into the darkness that she could still harvest DNA from his corpse, *that* sounded like an actual living nightmare.

He cleared his throat and managed to get his thoughts back in some semblance of order. "It's been forty years. Why now?"

Val shrugged. "Who knows? Time moves differently for vampires. We *do* age, but at such a decelerated speed that decades only feel like a year or two. Maybe the time got away from him, or maybe he was being careful not to be caught." Val glanced down at his phone, and a deep chill washed through Diego. Was Vampire Dave the one who had sent Val that anniversary text? Was he *taunting* him?

"Was it around Halloween? That it happened?" Diego prompted softly, and he swallowed down pure bitterness when Val nodded. *Happy anniversary, babe!*

"So, you can see why...letting him go, when he's as good as told me he's about to chain someone else up in his basement, seems extremely irresponsible. But what can I do to stop him by myself?"

It was a damn good question. But Val wasn't by himself, was he?

Not this time.

CHAPTER ELEVEN

The bread in the basket was all gone except the end piece, which Haley was avoiding because her mom had always liked the end pieces. Otherwise, it would have been consumed as a result of nerves long before, as the crumbs on the napkin in front of her could attest. She'd expected Leland to arrive fifteen minutes ago or more, but she hadn't heard a peep from him. And of course she didn't want him texting if he was driving, but if he'd left the office later than he'd expected, couldn't he have given her a heads-up? Now she was stuck just staring at her mother across a mostly empty breadbasket.

Had he chickened out on her? Had he decided hell no, their relationship wasn't nearly serious enough to be meeting her mom and now was planning to call it off?

"Did we need a few more minutes?" their waitress asked politely as she stopped by the table to refill their water glasses. She'd been very patient while they waited for their missing party member, but Haley could tell she was starting to write them off as a table that was going to get up and leave without ordering anything.

Still, going ahead and putting their order in felt rude, like she was giving up on Leland. Maybe a few more minutes.

"What do you think, Haley?" Kimberly Fern said from across the table. "Should we go ahead and order, maybe an appetizer?"

It was a reasonable suggestion, and a good compromise. But Haley felt a spike of hot embarrassment that her mother thought she had to guide Haley's response on the matter—and had, clearly, given up on Leland arriving.

"Yeah, we can go ahead and order," Haley said. "I'll give him a call and see if he's close, and if he wants me to put his order in."

"I'll give you a moment to make the call," their waitress said with a bland smile. "I'll be right back with some more bread."

Haley unlocked her phone as she'd been doing over and over the past few minutes, but this time she brought up Leland's contact and hit dial. It rang long enough that she was starting to think the network was down, but then his voicemail picked up. It wasn't a surprise, knowing Leland, that it was just the generic "The wireless customer you are trying to reach is not responding" message, but it was still unnerving.

She left a quick message, trying to sound cheerful and not impatient. But honestly, Leland had been acting weird ever since her mom had shown up and it was needling at her. He'd been fine when he found out she was a werewolf, but her mother being here was a step too far? *Sure. Fine. Whatever, Leland.*

"Everything all right?" Kimberly asked from across the table, breaking through Haley's mental fury. *Whew, deep breaths, Haley. Full moon's coming up, but that's no reason to lose your cool.*

"Yeah, just got his voicemail. I guess something must've come up."

It was probably only her imagination that her mother's expression was sympathetic, pitying. *Something must have come up* was a terrible excuse, and it always had been. It was how someone excused relationship problems without inviting discussion about them. But had she even been with Leland long enough for it to count as relationship problems?

"How's Dennis?" she asked, even though she had little to no interest in her mother's new boyfriend. Running off to Ohio with a bearded werewolf biker sounded like something teenage Haley would have done—but, well, she had to have gotten it from somewhere.

"He's fine." Kimberly sounded even less interested in discussing her dating life than Haley was. "But I wanted to ask you something—"

Haley's phone rang, the vibration nearly jolting it off the table. *Upham Co Sheriff.* What the heck? Leland was still at work? She had half a mind to let it go to voicemail, but she answered anyway, with an apologetic glance at her mother.

"Is this Haley Fern?" an unfamiliar voice on the other end said after her half-sarcastic greeting.

"Yes, this is," she answered, modulating her voice to sound more professional. *This is why you shouldn't let your temper get the better of you,* her inner voice said. Funny how it sounded so much like the woman sitting across the table from her. "May I ask who's calling?"

A rattle and scrape as the person on the other line went into a coughing fit, apparently covering the phone receiver. "Sorry 'bout that. This is Sheriff Rylan. We have your number on file as the contact for the Pine Grove Wildlife Preserve. That still accurate?"

"Yes, it is." Oh God. What happened? Was there something wrong with her forms? Had Leland not turned in the traffic control requisition form? Were they rejecting it because it was late? *Dang it, I knew I should've insisted on taking it up myself.*

"Sorry to be calling you out of the blue, ma'am, but as the liaison for the dedicated deputy, we wanted to let you know that Deputy Sommers is being put on paid leave for a few days. I reckon this might affect your plans for the town Halloween, so I wanted to let you know as soon as possible."

The words bounced around on the inside of her skull, and she stared at the breadcrumbs on the little saucer in front of her, unable to figure out how to answer. "Thank you for letting me know," she finally managed. "Is..." She stumbled over how to ask the question; it didn't sound like Leland's boss knew they were dating. Probably on purpose. "Is Deputy Sommers all right? What happened?"

"Had a bit of an accident in the county truck. He's all right, but he bumped his head pretty good. One of the boys is driving him to the doc to get checked out, but it shouldn't be anything worse than a big ol' headache. We'll let you know."

"I appreciate that." She gripped the phone tighter. Would Leland be able to answer her if she texted him? Was he—

"Oh, let me let you go. Getting another call, and I think it's his emergency contact calling me back. Don't hesitate to call if you need anything in the meantime."

"O-of course," she said to empty air as Rylan ended the call. She lowered the phone to her lap as her mother watched her with concern. Where to even start? Leland was late and hadn't answered because he'd had an accident—oh God, he hadn't been trying to answer her call, had he? Had *she* caused it? And now he wouldn't be able to help with Halloween, and she wasn't even his emergency contact...

"Everything all right?" Kimberly asked gently, and Haley shook herself. She felt like she ought to leave, to go help, but what could she do?

"I...Leland won't be here for lunch," she said, staring down at her phone. The rest of it sat swirling in her chest, a merry-go-round of new problems to solve.

CHAPTER TWELVE

IF THE JUICE BAR HAD SURPRISED HIM WITH ITS EAGER NEON, Roseblood swung so far in the other direction that it left him stunned. It was also dark, but that's where the similarities ended. Lush greenery dripped down emerald walls, uplit from the rich mahogany floor to cast eerie shadows on the dark blue ceiling. Around the edges of the room were chairs, chaises, and loveseats in tufted dark green leather, but right in the center was a long banquet table elegantly lit by the candles nestled among vases of sumptuous, heavy blossoms. Golden place settings gleamed in front of half the empty seats in an alternating pattern, and Diego suddenly understood why their business card had advertised the place as, *Exquisite dining for the refined palate.* Considerate, he felt, to offer food to someone whose blood you were about to drink.

Diego felt distinctly underdressed while they waited at the host stand, watching tall, slender people in dark suits and sleek dresses dripping with jewelry as they mingled, clearly waiting for something.

"Did you have a reservation?"

The voice startled him, but Val didn't seem surprised, turning toward the host who had appeared behind the stand. Fucking vampires and their ability to be almost completely silent, what with the no breathing and no pulse thing.

"We were invited," Val answered with a grave confidence Diego had never seen from him before. He handed over the card Tiffany had given them, a bold play. The back of the card read, *Present for admittance*, but who knew if it would work without their names on some kind of list.

"Hm." The host curled his lip, looking them up and down, but Val stared back, uncowed. It reminded Diego of the night they'd met, the way Val had sneered at him and called him *pup* in a bored, condescending tone. It had been a long time since Diego had seen him wield this smooth confidence, but wow, he could stand to see it more.

Finally, the host relented. "I suppose you may come in."

At both Hellebore and the Juice Bar, there had been at least one moment of feeling like a prime cut at a meat market, but Roseblood's patrons eyed him the way one might consider leftover meatloaf that had been dropped on the floor, which he felt was patently unfair. He'd put effort into his look tonight. So what if he wasn't wearing flawlessly tailored silk or—Jesus, was that woman's choker made of *real* rubies? Of *that* size?

Fuck. They didn't stand a chance.

"I don't think they're going to let us stay for dinner," Diego murmured as quietly as he could. They probably couldn't afford it anyway.

"Then we'd better start blending in," Val answered, leading him farther into the room.

Whereas the crowd at the Juice Bar was advertising in one way or another, Roseblood seemed like a place where everyone came prepared. *Strictly BYOB, I guess.* Gender, race, or physical appearance didn't seem to matter. The only thing they all had in common was their apparent wealth, and even then, Diego got the impression that one or two of the humans had been decked out and bejeweled by the vampires with them. In particular, one young woman who was bracketed by a doting couple seemed blushing and shy and completely out of her depth.

"We'll order off the menu for you, dear one," the female vampire was saying, stroking the girl's silky blonde hair. "Don't worry. We'll be sure you only have the finest dishes they serve."

"Will—what about you?" the girl worried, and the male vampire on her other side chuckled as he toyed with the thin strap of her white satin dress. Diego had a feeling that this pair had told her to wear white for the eventual dramatic effect.

"Don't worry about us, morsel," he chuckled. "We'll be perfectly happy tasting the decadence through you."

Well, *that* was something he'd never thought of. Huh. Diego leaned in close to Val and whispered, "Is that true? That you can taste what someone has eaten?"

Val shushed him softly, then angled toward a chaise in the back of the room. He held one hand out for Diego as he sank onto the leather, leaning back against the polished mahogany arm. Diego followed him, distracted by a glint in the back of the seat. *Oh my God*, the leather was tufted with chips of emerald, the dark stones catching a sultry sparkle from the candlelight and chandelier.

He had almost forgotten that he'd even asked Val a question by the time Val shifted so that their faces were almost touching and murmured in Diego's ear, "I've heard it's true, if the meal is recent enough, although some scientists think it's more smell than true taste."

"So that's the point of the banquet table then." Diego glanced toward the gleaming, every-other-seat place settings with a new understanding. "They're eating by proxy."

Val's fingers on his chin, turning his face away from the table, were softer than he would've strictly expected, and his heart gave one heavy thud in response. Val caught his breath, and Diego tried hard to relax, remembering Rayne's advice.

"Sorry." Val's hand fell away slowly. "But we should look like we know what we're doing here so we don't get chased out too early." He wet his lips and glanced over Diego's shoulder. "I haven't seen David yet. If he hasn't shown up by the dinner bell, we'll leave."

It took all of Diego's self-control not to turn and look at the table again. If David *was* there, would they stay through dinner? Would Val order from the menu and pick something *he* wanted to taste? Diego thought of the little scars on Rayne's neck and wondered again if it really did feel good to be bitten. To be fed on. He wasn't sure he wanted to find out...but he wasn't sure he *didn't*.

Val's palm sliding over his ribs sent an echoing shiver up his spine, and Val whispered an apology. "If we sit differently, you could see the room too," he said softly. "But it would be very...cozy."

Diego swallowed. "Well." He cleared his throat, then nodded. They had to commit to the bit after all. "All right."

Val lounged back against the arm of the chaise, stretching one leg out along the back like a spoiled housecat about to take a bath, and rested his elbows on the velvet cushion behind himself as he held one hand out to Diego to guide him— Oh. He was going to have to... All right. He could do this. What was the point of going to all this trouble if he chickened out because of a little cuddling? They were friends. It was fine.

Obediently, Diego lowered himself over Val's torso. He shifted to the side so his elbow wasn't digging into Val's stomach, but this just meant there was nowhere for his arm to go except behind the small of Val's back, into the narrow space between his body and the cushion. And there was nowhere for his hips to go that wasn't directly between Val's thighs. And there was nowhere for his head except cradled against Val's shoulder.

"A lovely pet you have there," the woman with the ruby choker said as she paused at the end of their chaise, and it was all Diego could do not to glare at her and sputter upright. "It's too bad he doesn't seem particularly comfortable. First time in a dinner club?"

"Yes," Val said, and that was the moment Diego felt fingers sifting through his hair—like someone might really pet their lapdog. "He's a bit shy, so we've only ever gone to private parties. Little get-togethers with friends, you know."

She nodded sympathetically. "Well, if I may offer some advice..." She leaned in and held her gloved hand up to her mouth as if she were imparting a secret. "Don't be afraid to use pheromones. I know some trainers like to call it cheating, but believe me, it works."

This close, Diego couldn't help but feel the twitch in Val's stomach muscles, but he maintained a smooth expression, a bored little smile, and his fingers didn't falter in Diego's hair.

"Thank you, I'll keep it in mind," Val purred. The vampire in red moved on, and Diego watched to see who she went to. Did she have a "pet" of her own? But if she did, she wasn't worried about keeping a particularly close eye on them.

"Don't worry," Val said, so quietly that if his mouth hadn't been at Diego's ear, even his werewolf hearing wouldn't have picked it up. "I won't use the pheromones on you."

"You can do that though?" Diego asked, making an effort to look relaxed, lest Miss Scarlett return with more unsolicited advice.

Val shrugged. "Vampires in general, yes. *I've* never done it." He paused. "Not...really."

Not really? What did that mean?

"Will anyone be suspicious if you don't?" Diego wondered aloud, their faces tucked close together so that they were barely speaking aloud, little more than whispers.

"It's really none of their business," Val said, quiet but firm, settling his hand over Diego's ribcage again.

Slowly, Diego became aware that there was soft music, piano and strings, and just under the edge of human hearing, barely noticeable to his werewolf ears, was...a heartbeat. "Do you hear that?" he asked Val. "The..."

"The mood music?" Val finally dropped his other hand from Diego's hair, and Diego felt wildly lightheaded, as if a heavy weight had been removed. "Yes."

Val didn't seem keen to elaborate, and Diego figured he had already been more talkative than most of the other nonvampire companions in the room. Maybe he ought to stop asking questions and just watch for Vampire Dave.

Val had done his best to describe David but had cautioned that his appearance might have changed. *Forty years isn't that long to a vampire, but even humans change a lot in five years.*

The idea that vampires did age, but more slowly, fascinated Diego. He'd kept Val up half the morning with questions. Did they get cavities? (Not really, but it was possible. Probably.) Did their hair turn gray? (Yes, but maybe not for hundreds of years, depending on how old they were when they were turned.) Could they die of old age? (Val had never heard of it happening.)

He had a million more. How did their decelerated aging affect psychological and emotional development? Would a vampire who was turned pre-puberty ever go through that change? Did their bodies even produce the necessary hormones the same way? But the truth was, Val didn't know the answer to most of them, and Diego had finally taken mercy on him.

Either way, it was wild to think that the man currently threading idle fingertips through Diego's hair had been in his early twenties over forty years ago and was now effectively in his mid-twenties. He'd have to ask Haley when he got back to Pine Grove if werewolves aged differently than humans. It would suck if they did, but the opposite way. What if werewolves aged in dog years and—

A familiar laugh out in the hallway ripped Diego from his wandering thoughts. He tensed, and Val immediately stopped petting him.

"What is it?"

It wasn't the same laugh though. It couldn't be. None of Diego's family knew he was here—in Vegas, much less in a high-end vampire dinner club—so how would they know to look for him? And if they weren't here looking for him, what were *they* doing in a high-end vampire dinner club?

"Your pulse is...elevated," Val murmured warningly, but there was another note underneath that Diego recognized. Hunger. "Try calming down."

But now Diego could smell...oh God, what was that? Salty and sweet all at once, thrumming along his senses, his tongue tingled with it when he inhaled deeply. He wanted to lick Val from his neck to his hips. He wanted to bare his throat and let Val do whatever he pleased. He *wanted.*

"Stop." Val's voice was quiet but desperate. "Diego, I need you to please calm down. I—I can't—"

Now that Diego thought of it, he hadn't seen Val drink one of his blood boxes before they'd left the motel. Was he hungry? Diego's pulse thudded again, deep and sweet, and this time two people turned to look at him—the woman in the ruby choker, of course, who looked smug, but also the male half of the couple with their white-clad blonde. The man's nostrils flared, and he smiled, fangs glinting—and just like that, Diego couldn't take his eyes off him, drawn like a magnet.

"No." Val tightened his hand in Diego's hair, pulling his face back around. Diego hadn't even realized he'd moved away. "Do not look at him," Val growled, and a confusion of arousal snapped through Diego. Was Val...jealous? "Don't look into his eyes for too long. That's how he gets inside your head."

A soft, golden chime shimmered through the room, and everyone's head turned at once. As soon as the other man's eyes left him, Diego felt the pressure ease. No one was looking at him anymore; the couple who had rung the bell had their attention.

An older white man stood at the podium, his arm around a smaller—younger?—man beside him. When the host emerged from the shadowy hallway to greet them, the taller of the two smiled.

"Apologies for our tardiness," he said in a smooth voice, and Val's hand tightened painfully on Diego's arm. He handed over a business card. "We were detained."

"I see." The host peered at the card, rubbing his thumb across the surface. "Come in and have a seat, please, while this is sorted."

"Your graciousness is appreciated." The man leaned over to speak to his companion, and when the two of them entered the dining lounge, Diego felt the air go out of the room.

Fuck. *Carlos*. What the *fuck* was his cousin doing here? Was that the familiar laughter he'd heard a minute ago? Diego knew his family wasn't supposed to know about weres or vamps or anything like that, but if Carlos was here, he either knew already or was in for a nasty surprise.

They'd never been that close—Carlos was Diego's only cousin on his dad's side, and he played nice for Guillermo's sake—but he was still family. Fuck, they'd never even talked enough for Diego to realize Carlos liked guys. What if he didn't? What if he was being manipulated with those stupid pheromones? Diego had to warn him—

"It's him." Val's nails dug into his arm, and Diego hissed at the bruise he could feel forming. "Diego, it's him. We have to go. Now."

"What? Who?" There was no way Val knew Carlos. But when Diego followed where Val was looking, he knew. The older white man who had entered with Diego's cousin following him like a puppy on a string—

"It's David."

CHAPTER THIRTEEN

Leland only felt a little guilty when he turned his phone ringer off. Haley had texted him just once—*The sheriff called, told me what happened. Are you ok?*—but Prudence wouldn't stop texting him. Apparently, Rylan had told *her* what had happened too, for some godforsaken reason. When he'd listed her as his emergency contact, this hadn't been the situation he'd had in mind. Maybe he ought to change it to someone who wouldn't give a shit, or who would at least be cool about it. Maybe Guerrera.

"You don't appear to be concussed," the doctor said, writing something on a prescription pad. "Your blood pressure's a little high, but that's not unexpected."

A little high felt like putting it mildly. His blood pressure had skyrocketed the minute he'd seen the hospital façade. He'd been too proud to protest that he couldn't afford it, but Donaldson had either read his body language or just knew what was coming.

"At least it happened on duty in the county truck," the man had said cheerfully as he'd parked. *"This is on the taxpayers' dime."*

The irony, of course, was that Leland had an even worse headache now than when he'd woken up—but at least he had two prescriptions for painkillers, even if he knew he wasn't going to fill them. "Some ibuprofen and some coffee, and some sleep, and I'll be fine," he said as he followed Donaldson back out to the parking lot.

"Course you will," Donaldson said. "You want to stop anywhere on the way back and get those scripts filled? Or pick up some ibuprofen?"

The automatic *no* died on his tongue, and he shrugged—and instantly regretted it when his shoulders seized. "Yeah. Guess so."

Donaldson tried to talk him into filling the prescriptions for something stronger—"Just to have in case it gets worse"—but he gave up after Leland made a noise at him that might have been an actual growl. Leland palmed four ibuprofen and dry-swallowed them on the way out of the store, though, and then tried not to think about anything on the drive home.

The light-blocking curtains in his apartment were the most expensive piece of furniture he owned, if they could be called that, and they were worth every penny. With Donaldson out the door, Leland crawled face-first into bed and closed his eyes in blessed, complete darkness.

When he woke again, it was to a soft bar of light illuminating a silhouette. He automatically reached for his firearm—which wasn't there. He had a dim memory of Donaldson locking it in his gun safe, which was maybe the smartest thing that man had ever done. And by the time he realized he was empty-handed, he recognized the blonde, backlit halo.

"What..." God, his mouth couldn't have been any drier if he'd shoveled some sand into it. "What're you doing here?"

"Well," Haley said, crossing her arms, her pretty mouth in a small, tight frown that made his palms sweat with guilt. "Seeing as I've heard from your boss *and* your sister twice in the past four hours, but hadn't heard a peep out of you, I thought I'd come make sure you hadn't slipped into a concussion-induced coma after all."

"My sister?" He sat up and tried to swallow, frowning when his throat ached. Damn, he wanted something to drink. "Pru called you...?"

"Rylan gave her my number, as your *professional liaison*," she said, and it might have just been the aftertaste of dry swallowing the ibuprofen, but she sounded so bitter he could damn near taste it. "I told her I'd come check on you, since you apparently haven't answered her, either."

"I told her I was fine," he grumbled, and she flinched.

"Well, I don't know what she was so worried about then. That's more than I heard." She sighed, uncrossing her arms and softening her posture, and it was Leland's turn to flinch. It was so much easier to deal with when she was angry. "Sorry, I don't mean to snap. I was just...worried. I didn't hear anything from you, and your boss said they were taking you to the hospital, and then you didn't answer..."

He should apologize. He might have been a stubborn ass who had never managed to keep a romantic partner for more than a month—shout-out to Kevin, who held the previous record at three and a half weeks when they were in middle school—but even he knew that the thing to do here was to apologize. For making her worry. For standing her up at lunch. For not answering her. For worrying Prudence enough that she'd called Haley.

But words weren't forming the way he needed them to, and he ended up just staring at her in silence. She stared back for long moments before she came closer, holding out her hand to touch his forehead—and he jerked away.

"Hey, whoa." She held both hands up, palms out, and took a step back from him. "I wasn't going to hurt you. I was just going to see if you had a fever."

"I'll be fine. I just need sleep." *Not helping, Leland. Fix it.* "Uh...what if I promise to call you in the morning?"

She narrowed her eyes but finally nodded. "All right. But if I don't hear from you by lunchtime, I'm coming over."

It wasn't until after she left that he realized he probably should have asked her for help getting food. He hadn't had more in his stomach all day than two cups of black coffee, and his body was starting to let him know about it.

He didn't have much in the kitchen, but there might be some bread and peanut butter. Maybe something in the freezer he could microwave. At that moment, he kind of wished he had his sister's affection for cheap, microwaveable ramen, but he could barely smell the stuff without wanting to vomit. It had been a lifesaver growing up though; a way to make sure Prudence had something to eat when all he could find to buy them food was a couple of handfuls of change in the couch cushions.

He hadn't been sick in almost that long either, and he hadn't gotten any better at it as time went on.

The box of Pop Tarts in the pantry had been there since before he'd moved in to the apartment, but how bad could it be? They were sealed, and full of preservatives besides. He didn't trust the toaster not to catch on fire—and didn't trust himself to be able to put it out right now if it did—so he ate them cold, washing down the cloying sweetness with a glass of tap water. All right. Maybe he was just hungry, but they weren't bad, and with some food in his stomach, he felt more able to face the volley of messages waiting on his phone.

Very first was an apology to Haley, a reiteration of his promise to call her in the morning, maybe take her and her mom out to breakfast as an apology. Next was Pru, who had texted him a grand total of thirty-four times. Good thing they didn't have to pay by the message anymore.

I'm fine. Just needed to get some rest. I'll text you again tomorrow, so you know I'm still all right.

She must have been practically sitting on her phone, waiting for a response after all these hours, because her response came through immediately.

OK. Be careful. Love you.

Damn, he'd be glad when he could get her out of that house.

All right, so that was taken care of. He could go to sleep now without the lingering guilt. Maybe after he brushed his teeth and drank another gallon of water. Jeez, maybe the headache had been dehydration all along. Wouldn't he feel like an idiot if he'd caused all this trouble by not drinking enough water?

His phone buzzed twice in succession while he was rinsing the toothpaste out of his mouth, and he chuckled. Haley, he guessed, probably negotiating a later time for breakfast.

But when he picked up his phone, they were from two different numbers.

Rylan: *I asked Meagher for a couple of extra officers to give you Halloween off. Sick time policy covers it.*

He frowned. No. For multiple reasons, he needed to be there on Halloween. He couldn't trust strangers with managing the tourists who had come to see Haley's pack, especially since Haley herself wouldn't be able to intervene. But whatever, he'd argue with Rylan tomorrow once he could prove he was feeling better.

He flipped back to find the second text, and immediately felt his chest burn with acid reflux. He probably shouldn't have eaten that Pop Tart after all. It definitely wasn't just because Mónica had texted him:

Niles is missing. Keep your eyes open.

Haley woke to the sound of her kitchen cabinets being opened and closed, pots and pans rattling, and her mother's familiar humming. The center of her chest ached, and she pulled the comforter tighter around herself. A glance at the clock showed six in the morning—her circadian rhythm was among the few things she *hadn't* inherited from her mother—and for just a minute, if she closed her eyes, she could almost believe she was a teenager, trying to catch five more minutes of sleep before she had to get up to drive to school.

She wasn't though. She was a grown woman and the alpha of her pack, and she needed to go over the logistics for who was going to be keeping the tourists in check now that her best human was out of the equation. The parking directors were easy enough. There were a couple of fields generously donated—for a small fee, of course—by the motel and by Sally and Luann. The RV park was already full.

The hard part was keeping the tourists from doing something stupid like trying to sneak away from the tour group and climb the fence into the preserve. While her pack wouldn't hurt them, the preserve was home to wild animals who would. Hopefully, the news of the "animal attack" that had unfortunately killed a local wildlife photographer back in the spring had made it far enough to scare them into behaving.

Which reminded her...Diego had promised to be back in time for the full moon, but she wished he would go ahead and get on with it. She'd like a chance to brief him, to maybe figure out how to ensure he didn't get separated from the pack. He'd been a werewolf long enough that being shifted should have started to feel like dreaming rather than just blacking out, but she'd still feel better if he didn't wander off by himself with a bunch of strangers around.

She thought about texting him, brought up the window and stared at the blinking cursor for a minute, then closed it with a sigh. Their deal had been he could have his sleepover with the vampires as long as he was back before the moon was up, and she would have to trust him. She felt like she owed him at least that much; it was his birthday after all, even if it did add another layer of stress to an already complicated night.

She groaned in frustration and dropped her phone to the bed, finally sitting up and finger combing her hair into place. Heck, maybe she'd ask her mom for advice. At the moment, she couldn't remember why she'd been so reluctant to do so from the beginning. Just dumb, empty pride, apparently.

"Do I hear a sunflower waking up?" Kimberly called from the kitchen, and Haley couldn't help a warm smile.

"That's an old one," Haley said as she shuffled out of the bedroom, pulling the cuffs of her sweatshirt down over her hands. Well. Leland's sweatshirt. "I don't think you've called me *sunflower* since ninth grade."

"No, not that long," Kimberly protested, but she sounded uncertain. She was standing in the middle of the kitchen, her hair in a messy bun, wearing rubber gloves, and Haley felt her blood pressure climbing. Had her mother been *cleaning*? What, so the full baseboard-wipe, sink-polish, refrigerator-scrub Haley had done just a couple of days ago wasn't good enough for her?

Sure enough, behind Kimberly on the counter was a bottle of disinfectant and a yellow sponge. What looked like a *new* yellow sponge, which meant Kimberly had gone looking for it. Gone were all the warm, fuzzy feelings of waking up to having her mother in the house again, and Haley had to count to ten just to keep her actual hackles from rising, the werewolf clawing its way to the paper-thin surface of her emotions.

She tried to sound politely concerned instead of humiliated and furious when she said, "You didn't have to clean, Mom. I know it's your old house, but you're here as a guest. I'd never ask you to clean."

"Oh, I know, honey." Kimberly laughed weakly, using her wrist to push a wayward curl out of her face. "You know me though. Can't sit still when I'm nervous or excited. I thought I'd clean up after my breakfast and got kind of carried away." She stripped the gloves off and laid them in the dish rack to dry. "Have you got anything else you need help with? Halloween prep? Laundry? Grocery shopping?"

Haley tried to make her smile look genuine, but her mother knew her well, and she could tell from Kimberly's expression that she hadn't quite pulled it off.

"Nope," she said with as much cheer as she could manage. "I'm good. Don't worry about a thing."

Kimberly's eyebrows drew together, and she opened her mouth, but instead of saying anything, she just nodded slowly. "All right. If you say so. Are you good if I take a shower?"

"Yeah, of course, go right ahead." Haley leaned against her freshly cleaned kitchen counters and inhaled the infuriating scent of fresh lemon. When the water came on in the bathroom, she dug a granola bar out of one of the cabinets and bit into it. Crumbs went all over her shirt, and she sighed. But halfway through the motion to brush them off, she stopped and instead knocked them into her hand and very carefully sprinkled a few onto the countertop and into the sink.

So there.

CHAPTER FOURTEEN

TIFFANY HAD BEEN DOWNRIGHT SMUG WHEN DIEGO HAD DEMANDED information on the alpha of the Las Vegas pack. *"I'm not doing this for you and your little turf war,"* he'd told her, and she'd just laughed.

"I don't really care why you're doing it. I get what I want, and that's all that matters to me."

Val had only stopped trying to talk him out of it once Diego had admitted that David's—date? dinner? victim?—was his cousin. He still wasn't happy about it, but he was back at the Blooming Sagebrush while Diego followed the GPS to the Main Drag for what was apparently a werewolf drag brunch. *Who knew?*

Maybe werewolves in Las Vegas had more fun than werewolves in Montana. Maybe Diego wouldn't hate his new life so much if he weren't living in the goddamn middle of nowhere with nothing interesting to do. Maybe once the tribunal was over, Haley would help him apply for a transfer to the Vegas pack like she'd promised so he could be close to home—and, apparently, go to drag brunches if he wanted!

Assuming he wasn't about to torpedo his chances of the Vegas alpha approving his transfer request by waltzing in here like he wasn't breaking probably a dozen werewolf rules he didn't know about. But he refused to think of himself as a trespasser in his own hometown. Fuck that colonizer shit.

But first, he needed coffee if he was going to stay awake long enough to even find this stupid fucking werewolf. So far, he hadn't seen anyone who fit the description—a couple of inches over six feet, blond, chiseled, etcetera. He sounded like he was going to be an ass, honestly. Just Diego's luck, he'd probably be one of those born-wolf supremacists like the ones who had ruined his life.

He sulked his way to a table, coffee clutched between both hands, and propped himself up on his elbows. God, it was almost eleven in the morning and he felt like he'd been up for days. They'd barely escaped Roseblood, their decision on whether to confront David made for them by Diego overhearing the maître d' discussing the legitimacy of their invitation with a manager in the back hall. But no sooner had they made it back to the car than Diego had demanded to talk to Tiffany.

There hadn't been time for more than a quick nap at the motel when he'd dropped Val off before coming here, but honestly, Diego had been too wired at the time and hadn't even tried. Now, however, he was wishing he had.

More coffee then.

The queen currently onstage was funny, some sleight of hand magic tricks and a regimen of bawdy jokes, but Diego's attention was elsewhere. He didn't even know the alpha's name—would Haley know? Surely if werewolves were such a rules-bound society, there was a database or something that she could look him up in.

But calling her to ask the name of the Las Vegas alpha might cause suspicion. Maybe he could frame it as trying to gather information for his eventual return home. Fuck, he was supposed to be back in Pine Grove today, by the timeline he'd given Michele, so he was going to have to come up with another cover story. Someone was bound to notice, and he hated lying to them, but it was too late to change any of that now.

Fine. *Fine!* He'd call Haley. He'd call her and tell her he'd be gone one more night and ask who the hell he should even be looking for in this damn club. And then once he'd gotten Tiffany's fucking meeting for her, he'd demand she do something about Vampire Dave. She was the archon's sister—surely she could throw him in vampire jail or get rid of him somehow.

He was about to press Call on his phone when the club's spotlight swung out over him, and he realized the queen onstage was pointing to him.

"Listen, honey, if you're making calls during my show, it better be to your sugar daddy," she cooed. "And if he's hot, you better let me talk to him."

Diego ended the call before it could even ring and tucked his phone away. "Sorry," he laughed, shrugging. Dammit. So much for flying under the radar. The queen made a show of pouting, then continued on, the spotlight swinging away from Diego. But before he could get his phone back out and try again, a small, long-haired man slipped into the seat next to him.

"Why are you here?" he asked in a low growl, and the hair on the back of Diego's neck stood up. That scent was unmistakable. He was a werewolf. But he didn't match the alpha's description, and Diego *had* to talk to the alpha, not some lycanthropic bouncer. He couldn't let this guy run him off.

"I'm here to watch the show, man," he lied. "I won't get my phone out again. What's the big deal?"

"You're not from here." Jeez, for all that this guy was probably a full inch shorter than Diego, he was intimidating. "Why are you here?"

And then Diego had a brilliant, wonderful idea. "Why don't you run tell your alpha," he taunted, grinning. "Tell him to come threaten me himself."

"I will, as soon as his show's over." A sharp, crooked grin and a glance up at the leggy blonde onstage. Oh damn, the Vegas pack really *did* have more fun. "And if you'd rather us *not* tear you limb from limb, you could get out of our territory. If you hurry, you might make it before we catch up with you—and pray that if we *do*, you get to deal with my husband instead of me."

"Your—" Diego sat up straight. "The alpha is your husband? Listen. I need to talk to him. The vampires—"

A burst of applause drowned him out, but Diego saw the way the man's expression hardened at the word *vampires.* Shit. And for being a small man, the alpha's husband had a grip like iron; Diego could feel his arm bruising as he was hauled out of his chair and dragged toward the back door of the club. He stumbled as he was pushed into the alley but stayed on his feet, whirling to fight—and stopped as he saw the blonde drag queen step out behind the shorter man. The wig was gone, the playful queen demeanor dropped, and instead a very buff alpha in a gold sequin dress and honestly impressive stiletto heels was glaring at him.

"Corbin?" the alpha said, and the smaller man—his husband, Corbin, apparently—gestured to Diego.

"He said he needs to talk to you. Something about the vampires."

The alpha raised one eyebrow and crossed his arms. "An unregistered werewolf, barging into my place of employment to blab about the vampires right out in the open? Two strikes right off the bat."

Diego rolled his eyes, fury boiling up in him. "I'm not—fucking Christ, I'm not *unregistered.* I'm not a *dog.* What, are you going to ask to see my papers next?"

The alpha snarled, but Corbin put his hand on his husband's arm. "It was an unfortunate choice of words," Corbin said quietly. "But we didn't receive a request for a new werewolf in the territory, and there have been...troublemakers."

"No shit," Diego huffed, automatically reaching up to rub at the scar on his shoulder from his own run-in with so-called *troublemakers.* All right, all right. If the Vegas pack had been having issues with those assholes, then maybe he could understand their hair-trigger reaction. And he *was* breaking the rules, technically. Even if they were stupid-ass rules. "I'm here with a friend. It's...a long story, but we need your help. He needs the archon to control one of his coven members who's hurting people." He hesitated; he didn't want to give too much of Val's personal history away to these strangers. Especially not strangers who used words like *unregistered* to refer to people. Werewolves, whatever. "The archon's sister said we had to do her a favor first, and the favor is that she wants to talk to you. She said she wants an alliance."

He took a deep breath; all of that sounded stupid when he said it aloud, but it was what he had.

"Fuck the vampires." The alpha's lip curled with the declaration, and his husband sighed.

"Apollo, if they want an alliance..."

"And you think they're telling the truth?" Apollo shook his head. "I'm sorry about your friend. But vampires don't keep promises. They break them every time. You and your friend should go home and forget about it. If you leave by tonight, I'll..." He frowned. "I won't report your trespass."

Diego couldn't help thinking of Haley, of how determined she always was to make something work, how she always tried to find the path that would benefit everyone involved. She wouldn't use this weak-ass excuse of vampires being promise breakers to simply not...try. God. What kind of asshole did this alpha think he was, that he wouldn't even *try*?

"Yeah, well, fuck you too," Diego snapped. "There's an empty parking lot here." He thrust out the Hellebore business card with an address scribbled on it. "We'll be there tonight. So will Tiffany, if you decide you want to stop being a dick and come at least talk to her."

Apollo's frown deepened. "If you're still here tonight, I *will* report you to the regional alpha and have you disciplined."

When Apollo didn't take the card from him, Diego dropped it on the ground between them and flipped up his middle finger.

"Well, then you're a dick *and* an asshole, so I guess you can go fuck yourself."

They didn't try to stop him from leaving, and as far as he could tell, they didn't follow him to the parking lot and that was farther than he'd thought he would get. So much for the Vegas pack being a better fit for him.

Honestly, so far the worst part about being a werewolf was the other goddamn werewolves. Haley was all right, and the Pine Grove pack was friendly enough—almost enough to make up for living in the middle of fucking nowhere—but all the rest of them had been awful, and if that was the kind of thing he had to look forward to for the rest of his existence, he was going to be really fucking pissed about it.

He was still steamed when he got back to the motel room, and it wasn't until after the door slammed dramatically behind him that he remembered that it was daylight. *Fuck*. But Val's bed was empty and—oh, the door to the bathroom was closed.

Should he knock? Should he tell Val he was back? It was way past Val's bedtime, and Diego didn't want to disturb him if he was already asleep, but also...there was only the one bathroom. Diego was going to need it at some point. The coffee he'd had at the Main Drag would make sure of that. Ugh, fine. He wasn't having a good day, and Val could be miserable with him.

The door opened before he could knock, though, and Val peered up at him from the tile floor, propped up against the wall.

"From the general door-slamminess and huffing and puffing and blowing the house down, I presume your visit to the big bad werewolf didn't go anywhere."

"Well, he's not turning me over to border control yet at least," Diego grumbled. Territory lines—what fucking bullshit. He took Val's implicit invitation and stepped into the bathroom, sinking down onto the floor, back braced against the sink pedestal. "But he wasn't interested in hearing about any truce with the vampires, and he said if I'm not out of here by tonight, he'll alert the authorities."

Val's eyebrows went up. "Which means if we show up at the meeting place, he'll probably show up too, if only to hunt you down."

"Comforting thought. But yeah, at least he'd be there, and that's all we promised Tiffany. A meeting, not necessarily a ceasefire."

But all she'd promised them in turn was David's location, not her assistance in dealing with him, and they were almost out of time. He was going to have to drive back to Montana during the day as it was and just hope he could stay awake. He still wasn't able to fully control himself while he was shifted, and he'd much rather be with a pack that knew him and would look out for him than here in Vegas or—God forbid—somewhere on the highway.

Diego leaned his head back against the porcelain sink with a heavy sigh, and out of the corner of his eye he noticed Val's cooler with the lid off. He could see just one blood pack inside, and he sat up sharply.

"When's the last time you ate?"

Val's gaze darted away from his. "Uh. Before Roseblood, I had a little bit. I was afraid I'd lose control in that atmosphere if I was too hungry, but this is my last pack."

"Is that gonna be enough?" Diego gestured to his cooler, and Val closed the lid. "We still have to get through today, tomorrow, and the drive home."

"I'll be all right. When I realized we were going to have to stay, I started rationing. You don't have to worry about me hurting you."

"I'm not." And it was true; it had not crossed Diego's mind to be worried about Val hurting him, not even if he was hungry. Maybe he was being naïve; maybe Val *would* injure him if he went into a blood haze, but it didn't seem possible. "But...you know, you have a source of fresh, free blood very close by."

At Val's raised eyebrow, Diego pointed to himself. He thought of Rayne, of a club full of people desperate to be bitten, and wondered once again if he would like it. It did seem intimate, in a way, offering part of himself to keep someone else alive...

"Absolutely *not*." Val physically recoiled at the suggestion, and Diego frowned.

Rude. "I know you don't really like to live-feed, and I know I smell like a werewolf, but—"

"No." Val shook his head. "I won't bite you." His jaw worked silently for a moment, and Diego realized Val was pressing his tongue to the tip of one of his canines. His skin tingled; he nearly shivered. What would Val's fangs look like fully extended? "I've only ever bitten someone once, and it was—it was awful."

"But if there's no other option—"

"I'll be fine." Val pushed the lid on the cooler closed even tighter, then used it as leverage to get to his feet. Diego didn't think he was imagining that Val's hands and legs were both trembling. "But now that you're back, let's...well, let's get some sleep before we have to be up to go to the meeting. Like you said, we have a long couple of days ahead of us."

CHAPTER FIFTEEN

Leland felt better. For the first time in twenty-four hours, he could sit up without feeling like his head was going to roll off his shoulders. A headache still pressed at the inside of his temples, and his skin felt tender all over, but he was better.

But Halloween was day after tomorrow. Which meant he needed to get dressed—no, first, get a shower. Then get dressed, take Haley to breakfast, and march up to Rylan's office to tell him he was taking over crowd control at Halloween again, if Leland had anything to say about it.

Which he didn't. By the time he got out of the shower, his muscles felt like they'd been run through a blender, and he had to lean his head against the tiles for almost two whole minutes.

Okay. Dammit. Maybe he wasn't fine. But he'd promised Haley breakfast this morning, and after ditching her twice in a row, he wasn't keen to do it again. If he took his time and didn't push himself too hard, he'd be fine. And hell, maybe he'd feel back to normal after eating.

Even getting downstairs cast doubt on that though. The stairs were hard to manage, his knees weak and joints sore, his hand braced on the wall paneling to steady himself. He hobbled the few steps across the sidewalk to his Chevy and had to stop before hauling open the heavy door. Just one more minute. Then he'd go.

"Hey, handsome." A car door shutting close behind him startled him into awareness—had he dozed off leaning on the truck? He looked up to find Haley coming toward him with two cups of coffee in her hands. "You look like you could use a pick-me-up. Actually, you kinda look like you could just stand to be picked up."

"Am I late?" He didn't think he was late for their breakfast date. He'd been keeping an eye on the clock all morning. "What are you doing here?"

"Mom's an early riser, got me out of the house ahead of schedule. So, we thought we could come pick you up instead."

We? Oh no. That meant... He looked over to see Haley's mother in the driver's seat of the rental car. She waved at him as soon as they made eye contact.

"I don't think I'm making a good impression on your mom," he said, frowning. Haley set both cups of coffee down on the hood of his truck; her hands were still warm when she skimmed them over his back.

"I'm pretty sure she understands that people get sick sometimes." She rubbed across the backs of his shoulders, and he felt himself relaxing into it. He hadn't realized how sore he felt; maybe that was left over from running the truck off the road. "I think you might have the flu, honey."

"No." The denial was automatic, even though part of him knew she was probably right. He'd gotten whatever it was Rylan had, most likely—but even if that was true, it wouldn't make a difference. He'd only stayed home from school *once* when he was sick, and he'd regretted every minute of it. After that, he'd learned to just push through, and that's what he'd do this time. "I'll be fine."

He couldn't *see* her roll her eyes, but he heard her scoff and knew that was what she was doing.

"I know you'll be fine, but you'll get there a lot faster if you get some more rest. Come on, I'll help you back upstairs. Let me just tell Mom I'll be right back."

In the time it took Haley to explain the situation to her mother, Leland felt most of the rest of the strength he'd gathered melt away. It was frustrating as hell, but it also meant he didn't have the energy to argue about it when Haley slung his arm over her shoulder and turned toward the stairs up to his apartment.

They got up two steps before she stopped.

"Leland..." She hesitated like she knew he wasn't going to like whatever she said next. "What if I take you to my house?"

"...What?"

"For one, there aren't as many stairs at my house. For two, I can... well, I've got a few things I have to finish, but I can look in on you. And keep an eye on you at night."

"Don't want you getting sick too," he mumbled. He had no idea what a werewolf with the flu looked like, but it probably wasn't pretty.

"I'll be fine." Well, now that the tables were turned, he realized how annoying that phrase was. No wonder she'd looked like she wanted to thump him when he said it. "C'mon. Let's load you up in the car. You can sleep in my bedroom. If it makes you feel better, I'll sleep in the guest room with Mom."

The ten-minute drive to Haley's was a blur. He had a vague memory of apologizing to Haley's mom on the way—maybe more than once, if her tone was anything to go by when she said, "It's no trouble at all," while she put the car into park.

He hated to admit it, but he felt better the second his boot touched Haley's front porch. He still felt sick as a dog, but underneath was the warmth of a safety net. He did his best to help her as she got him undressed and into bed, but he was getting clumsier by the minute.

Even as she tucked him under the blankets, which Leland was absolutely going to get up from just as soon as he rested for one more second, he could see Haley practically twitching with impatience. Halloween was in two days, and they both had things to do.

"After I get a nap, I'll help you with the—" What did she even have left to do for Halloween? He had no idea. "The stuff."

"I'm more worried about you, Le," she said, frowning. "I'm gonna ask Karen to look in on you." She bit her lip, fidgeting. "Or...or, if you aren't feeling better by Halloween, I guess, Mom could lead the run, and...I mean, I'd be a wolf, but I could stay here with you—"

"Absolutely not." Leland levered himself upright, then had to pause while the room spun and everything turned upside down for a second. When he managed to open his eyes again, Haley had her arms crossed tightly over her ribs, and an instinctive jolt of something dark and bitter lanced through him. "You've got work to do. Don't worry about me."

"Leland, I just peeled you off the side of your truck. I had to practically carry you into the house. I know you don't have any groceries in your house and probably haven't eaten, so I'm gonna get you some food. What do you want, orange juice and chicken soup?"

The bitter feeling in his stomach turned instantly to nausea, and he shook his head, swallowing the bile. "No. I—not that."

Struggling out from under the flannel sheets—hot soup and cold juice soaking through the fabric, through his shirt and shorts, his father's voice echoing off the walls as the bowl clattered somewhere close to his mother's feet—broken glass—

"Okay. What do you like when you're sick then?"

To be left alone. He barely held back the uncharitable comment; Haley didn't deserve that. "Nothing." *Go away.*

Illness was vulnerability. Illness meant a weak spot to exploit. He didn't have the luxury of being sick, and Haley standing there worrying about him when he knew very well she had a full schedule of things to get done was making him antsy.

"Uh huh." Haley sighed. "Well, I'm going to bring you some food anyway. Mom and I will figure something out that isn't orange juice or chicken soup."

Leland wished he had it in him to argue, but she leaned over and pressed a kiss to the center of his forehead, and all the fight went out of him at once. He closed his eyes and let the mattress swallow him.

CHAPTER SIXTEEN

Even in his dreams, Diego was exhausted. Arms like lead, too heavy to lift when cool, dry kisses trailed down his jaw, too clumsy to wrap around the dark shadow that arched over him. Beyond the inky silhouette, he could see softly glowing lights shifting shades between ruby and emerald, and he could feel his own pulse heavy in his veins, the deep thrumming of desire.

Was he tired, or was it something else that kept him laid out on the chaise? It had been a very long time since he'd been touched like this, the shadow's hand firm but tender as it skated down his body. He anticipated the iron grip on his wrists, the way his hands were pinned over his head, the slow lick of a tongue across his throat, and the gleam of fangs in the shadows.

He knew he ought to be frightened, but he would've known that scent anywhere—faint, expensive cologne and dry earth—and it was impossible to be afraid of the vampire behind it, even when those fangs scraped over his skin, slowly, tantalizingly... And then the piercing pain as they sank into his neck as easily as if he were a ripe plum. The electric jolt catapulted him out of sleep, and he groaned and rolled onto his stomach, burying his face in the pillow.

His skin crawled like it was trying to heave him out of his own body, muscle and bone. His dreams still clung to him, and he was moments away from doing something incredibly stupid, like climbing into Val's bed and—

No, dammit, it's just the full fucking moon. It's not real. You're just horny.

But even though he knew that, Diego wanted to rub himself all over Val Viktor Kunes, which was possibly the weirdest thought he'd ever had since becoming a werewolf, and definitely weirder than anything he'd ever thought of before. Val was still out cold, and according to the clock, they had about an hour before he needed to change that.

A whole hour.

Fuck it, he wasn't going to last an hour in this tiny room with Val's scent hanging in the air. Full moon or genuine attraction, it didn't matter; Diego only had so much self-control. Unfortunately, he also couldn't leave. The sun was still up, and he couldn't endanger Val by opening the door like it was nothing. There was only one place to go, and Diego could only hope that stretching out on the cold bathroom tiles would cool him off.

It didn't.

In the middle of the day, with the bathroom door between them, it was all he could do not to whine and try to dig his way under the crack in the door to get to that scent. Holy shit, it had to be the cologne, right? That couldn't be just the pure smell of Val lighting up all his primal instincts, could it? He'd never thought cool, earthy aromas could make him want to hump a pillow, but here he was.

He clenched his hands between his thighs and took deep, long breaths as he tried to think about literally anything except how much he wanted to be touched and how much he needed it to be done by a very specific person instead of his own hand. He was dimly aware of time crawling by, the magnetic pull of sunset approaching. He could tell the moon was waxing, that it was almost full, by how keenly he felt the day shifting into night without even being able to see the sky.

"Pup?"

Rage at the nickname and arousal at the soft-rough tone of Val's voice outside the door flooded Diego with fight-or-flight adrenaline, and he ground his teeth and stared at the wall, counting his breaths to try to get himself under control before he answered.

"...Diego?"

Two deep breaths as he tilted his head back, and a death glare burning a hole in the fucking ceiling and the brown water spot just above the toilet. "Yeah. I'm here."

"Yeah, I—" A little rustling noise on the other side of the door, then a soft thump and the movement of shadows under the door told Diego Val had sat down against it, their bodies pressing against opposite sides of the flimsy barrier. "I know you're there. I can hear your heartbeat."

Of course he could.

"I can leave the room. If you need to sleep."

"No, that's not..." Val's sigh grated his nerves. "Are you okay?"

Well, there was a million-dollar question. Was he? "I'm not hurt."

A long, drawn-out silence pressed against every bit of self-control Diego had, until Val finally said, "That's not what I asked."

"I'll be fine." He only had to stick this out for a couple more days. One way or another, things would be over by Halloween. By his birthday. God. Had he even told Val it would be his birthday? Did it matter?

"Is it..." Val's hesitation was so loud Diego could feel it pressing at his eardrums. "Could I get the cooler whenever you're finished? I want to make sure I'm not going to this meeting on an empty stomach."

Well, there was no chance in hell he was going to jack himself off if Val was awake with the world's thinnest door between them, so by definition, he was finished. He reached up to turn the handle, letting the door swing open.

The reversal of their earlier positions wasn't lost on Diego, nor was the way Val's nostrils flared and pupils dilated the moment he entered the room. It sent a surge of power through Diego that rattled his bones and made his teeth ache, and as Val crouched beside him to open the cooler, the dark room grew lighter and lighter. It was only Val's sharp intake of breath that made him realize he was partially shifted, the wolf inside pushing to the surface to take what it wanted that Diego wasn't giving it.

And then—that salty-sweet fragrance from before, the one that had made him feel like the air itself was intoxicating, like he could swim in it. If Diego had been overwhelmed by the scent at Roseblood, the wolf was practically salivating now.

"I need you to calm down," Val murmured, sounding like he was right at Diego's ear.

"Are you using pheromones on me?" Diego asked breathlessly, and Val frowned.

"No. Maybe. Not on purpose. But your pulse—"

"It's because you smell good." Oh, he did. Even without the strange new depth that the wolf was finding in the fragrance, Val always smelled good.

"That's just—it's a trick." Val huffed. "It's not real, Diego. It's a lie. It's the same kind of biological lie that—"

He seemed to realize his voice was rising, and he cut himself off, dragging a hand across his face.

"It's not," Diego rasped. "It's not the same as what David did to you. You aren't tricking me." A visible tremor in his fingers as he reached for Val made him clench his fist and withdraw without touching him. "The pheromones...they're a reaction, aren't they?"

Val closed his eyes, looking pained, but he nodded slowly. "Yes. We can emit pheromones deliberately, but they happen naturally when we... want something. Someone."

"Is that what you meant, in Roseblood?" Diego asked quietly. "That you hadn't *really* used them on anyone before?"

Val looked away. "Yes. But I don't...I'll tell you about it someday. But not today. It's harder to stay in control right now, and I can't..."

This time, not even his trembling fingers could stop Diego from sliding his hand across Val's arm, comforting and coaxing all at once. "Is it harder because you're hungry?"

"I'm not feeding from you, Diego." Val's voice was hard and unyielding, but his eyes were desperate. "Please. Don't ask me to, not like this." He turned his hand up to Diego's touch, their palms rasping together. "I don't want you to see me like that, like an animal who can't control myself."

Diego's laugh sounded hollow even to his own ears, the echo plinking sadly off the bathroom tiles. "Don't forget who you're talking to. For five months now, I've turned into an actual animal every full moon, and until last month, I had no idea who I was the whole time. Hell, I might've killed someone the first time! We don't know." He tried to pull his hand away, but Val's fingers tightened around his. "And tomorrow night, it's going to happen again."

"Di, I didn't..." Val's thumb skimmed across his palm. "I'm sorry. I didn't mean it like that. It just..." He sighed. "I don't like doing it. It reminds me of D-David, and the first few horrible weeks of not knowing how to survive as a vampire. I hurt people. I didn't mean to, but I did. And I don't want to hurt you." His smile was sad, and Diego's heart nearly pounded through his chest when Val lifted their hands together and pressed a single, apologetic kiss to Diego's palm.

That's not helping the elevated pulse thing, Diego almost said, but the joke died on his tongue when Val's dark gaze met his through lowered eyelashes, and his fingers curled against Val's jaw instead.

"I don't want to hurt you either," Diego whispered, and Val drew back just a little.

"Pup, I hardly think—"

"I don't mean like that." Diego swallowed. "It's the full moon tomorrow night. Maybe someone who's been a werewolf longer would be able to tell if what they were feeling was real or the moon, but..." He brushed his thumb along Val's lower lip. "But what if three days from now, when the moon is waning and you aren't hungry anymore, we regret this? And then it's awkward, and I'll..." His throat tightened, and he cleared it roughly. "And then I'd have ruined the best friendship I've had in years."

Val's mouth twisted into a regretful smile. "I'd like to think we'd manage, and it would just be something we'd laugh about every now and then." He kissed Diego's thumb. "But I can't exactly argue with you without being a massive hypocrite."

"Listen, I..." Out in the room, two alarms started beeping at once. Diego recognized one as his own phone; the other must have been the hotel clock. Either that or Val had downloaded a truly heinous alarm tone.

"We need to go if we're going to meet Tiffany," Val said, dropping Diego's hand, and Diego flexed his fingers against the sudden emptiness. "Let's pack the car with as much as we can. We're...probably going to have to drive through the night to get you back in time."

Assuming Apollo and Corbin didn't kill him or show up with the werewolf police or something. And if they did, well, it would still be nice to have all their things in the car so they wouldn't have to try to go back to the hotel while being chased.

"You'd better finish that off before we go," Diego said, gesturing to the last blood pack in the cooler. He wasn't sure how much was left in it, if Val had been rationing it. From the amount of time Val drank through the straw before it started crinkling, visibly empty, it wasn't much.

Damn, he really hoped they didn't have to fight their way out tonight.

CHAPTER SEVENTEEN

"Everywhere is full," Luann shouted cheerfully as she put Haley's to-go order in a plastic bag. Not that Haley needed to be told; there hadn't even been an empty spot to park outside the diner. Her Range Rover was perched half on, half off the road, and there were plenty of other vehicles parked along the shoulder and even into the ditch. Leland would have opinions, if he weren't currently dead to the world in Haley's bed. "Somebody said the Halloween run 'went viral,' whatever that means. Deputy's gonna have his work cut out for him tomorrow!"

Ah, jeez. Maybe Leland would be awake when she got home and could fill her in on the situation with the traffic and crowd control officers, now that he was out of commission. Not that she'd let on to him, but she wasn't too happy about not having an ally among the law enforcement who knew what was going on. Walker and Donaldson she knew from past Halloweens, of course. They'd come down to help George with the parking and traffic control most years. But they both thought the werewolf pack was some hokey local legend played up for tourists, and Haley wasn't in a hurry to tell them otherwise.

This year, though, she'd been hoping Leland could keep an eye out for any assholes that might have sneaked in. She had a new wolf to look out for and a *lot* of strangers in town. She'd hoped for maybe fifty to a hundred semi-locals from neighboring towns; exactly how "viral" had they gone? What kind of people had it attracted? The last thing she needed was some social media influencer who thought flagrantly breaking the rules was good for their views.

She didn't trust the other deputies to take it seriously; there was a lot of "boys will be boys" nonsense she'd heard them spout when she was younger. Any other year, she would've just stayed human and let someone else lead the pack, but this year there was no staying human for anyone. The full moon was going to turn them all as soon as it had risen completely over the horizon.

"Thanks, Luann," Haley said, taking the food and heading toward the door. She had to squeeze past two girls taking selfies on their phone and nearly fell over the back of one of the booths, where an enterprising couple had set up with a small camera and a fuzz-covered microphone.

"...here in tiny Pine Grove, Montana, where the locals have an unusual Halloween custom. We'll have more details for you later, but if you'd like to see more of what we're doing on this channel, make like a werewolf and like and subscribe!"

Haley groaned and finally managed to squeeze out the door without compromising the food. Dang it, she wasn't going to be able to do this alone. If she had even just *one* other person—Jo or Leland or Michele—she would probably be okay. But she really, *really* did not need for some influencer with a YouTube channel to get too close to the pack and realize that the big, hulking alpha who was the grand finale wasn't, in fact, special effects or a guy in a suit. Hiding in the open worked for Pine Grove, but Julio would have her head if her pack hecked it up for everybody.

Not to mention if somebody spooked Diego, just when he was starting to get through the worst part of being a werewolf. They were already going to have to go to a whole tribunal about someone he *might* have hurt or killed in the throes of his first transformation; she absolutely did not need video of him attacking someone to hit the internet.

The whole way home, it sat in her chest like a dropped barbell. She'd been worried about Halloween not having enough attendance this year. She hadn't bet on it being too much to handle. As she started setting the takeout containers on the cabinet, hesitating over how to take Leland's food to him, she heard quiet footsteps and a softly cleared throat in the kitchen doorway.

She turned, flashing an automatic smile at her mother. "Hey, Mom. Sorry it took me a minute. Luann's was overrun." She tapped one of the boxes. "This one should be your omelet."

"Thanks for getting food," Kimberly said, slowly coming to stand beside her. She took the box but didn't open it, hands perched awkwardly on the lid. She was wearing a ring with a small stone on her left hand, and Haley couldn't help but think it looked strange. "Leland was still out when I checked on him."

"Thanks for checking on him." Haley hesitated, then nodded at the ring. "Dennis proposed? Or you did?"

"Oh. Not officially." Kimberly twisted the ring almost nervously. "This was more of a...planning to propose. Probably."

Haley couldn't help chuckling. "How old are you now?" she teased. "I guess it's never too late to have a promise ring."

Kimberly shook her head. "Honestly, Dennis probably would've gone the whole nine yards. I guess more accurately this ring is *I promise to think about maybe getting engaged someday*."

"Ah." Haley's smile turned warm and fond. "There's the Mom I know. Never in a hurry to make a commitment."

"What about you?" Kimberly stopped fiddling with her ring to pin a look on Haley. "I never heard a peep out of you about getting engaged, not even with Jessie, and you lived with him for two years. And what about Leland?"

"I don't think I could've married Jessie," Haley laughed, dodging the second question. "It wasn't that kind of thing. Anyway. Assuming I get through Halloween alive, we can revisit the topic."

"Fair enough." Kimberly took a deep breath and held it for a minute. "I'm...aware that asking you this could potentially be upsetting, but I want you to know that I'm only bringing it up because I care about you."

Oh boy. Nothing good ever came with that kind of preface. "All right,"

Haley said slowly. "Shoot." She was ready for anything, any kind of criticism, any advice or passive aggressive remark or—

"I...are you all right, baby?"

—anything but that.

To her absolute horror, the soft, genuine question seeped into all the cracks Haley had been desperately trying to hold together for days now. Maybe weeks, maybe months. It welled up inside her until she was blinking burning eyes and pressing her lips together in an attempt not to just cry.

"I'm all right," she croaked, then laughed wetly at how absolutely unconvincing that had sounded. "I mean—sure, I'm stressed. There's so much to do, and now that Leland's sick, I'm going to have to depend on strangers to make sure the tourists don't do anything to endanger the pack, and I'm worried I should be doing more to help out in town, and I'm worried I should be doing more to take care of Leland, and I'm worried about Diego, but I don't want him to feel like I'm hovering or controlling or that I don't trust him..."

She stopped to take a breath and shook her head.

"Anyway. I'll be fine, it's just that...anybody I could ask for help isn't available. Jo has newborns, Michele is in South Dakota with her uncle, Leland is..." Haley glanced over her shoulder toward the bedroom. "So, it's a little harder than I thought it'd be."

"That's understandable. Especially the part where you don't want Diego to feel like you don't trust him. I know that feeling very well."

Haley laughed around a sniffle, dashing her wrist under her nose. "Are you trying to tell me something?"

"I'm trying to tell you that I'm afraid that if I offer to help, it will sound like I don't think you can handle this. And I absolutely think that you can handle it as well as anyone else could, but everyone needs help sometimes."

"*You* never did." Haley was aware she sounded bitter and petty. "This pack would've kept electing you alpha until you died. They just settled for me because you moved to Ohio."

Kimberly's hands on Haley's shoulders were warm and firm in a way she hadn't realized she'd missed. How long had it been since they'd really spent any time together, much less had a conversation like this?

"There are at least two wrong statements there," Kimberly said gently. "They didn't *settle* for you. You are every bit as qualified for this position as anyone else. Heck, you might be *more* qualified than I was when I first took over." She rubbed her thumbs over Haley's upper arms and offered a tiny smile. "And yes, I also needed help. I *had* help. Julio spent so much time with this pack because I needed the extra support, and then once Tania took over, she did too."

"But I never..." Haley shook her head, frowning. "I never saw any of that."

"I tried not to let you see the places where I needed support because I didn't want you to feel like you had to step up and fill that role. You were a child. You deserved to live your life without feeling like you had to help me fix mine."

"That..." Haley took a deep breath. "I can understand that. And in that case, I'm not sure exactly what help I need with this, but I would be very grateful if we could figure that out together."

"We can start with me telling you that I promise you every business in Pine Grove will be fine without you trying to help manage the flood of customers, so you can mark that off your list of worries. None of them are shy about asking for things if they need it."

"That's honestly a relief." Haley shuddered. "I barely made it back from town. Did you know," she said as she started pulling plates down out of the cabinet, "there were at least *three* streamers in Luann's today? One of them was talking into a camera and had this weird sign-off. I guess it was supposed to be a joke, but I didn't get it."

"What was it?" Kimberly finally opened her box and used a fork to slide the omelet inside out onto a plate.

Haley wrinkled her nose as she tried to recall the exact wording. "I dunno, it was something like..." She affected a deep voice. "'Be like a werewolf and like and subscribe.' Are werewolves even known for sub— Why are you laughing?"

"Lycan," Kimberly said between giggles. "Be like a werewolf and *Lycan* subscribe."

"Oh, for..." Haley snorted. "That's the worst joke I've heard since you moved to Columbus."

Kimberly's answering cackle sounded absolutely delighted, and Haley had to admit that for the first time in days, she was feeling optimistic. Maybe they stood a chance of getting through this in one piece.

CHAPTER EIGHTEEN

DIEGO KNEW THAT HE WASN'T THE MOST PATIENT PERSON, EVEN without the full moon stirring him into a simmering ball of hormones and rage, but turning up to the address Tiffany had given them only to find the parking lot teeming with scene kids would've tested the patience of a saint, he felt.

"Well, now what the fuck do we do?" He gestured out the windshield at the mass of writhing bodies, the thump of the bass rattling the Audi's windows. He was sure they didn't have a permit either, which just meant someone was going to call the cops on a noise complaint.

No matter how bullshit Diego thought that was, it was still a real danger. And they were fucked if the cops started asking for IDs; Val's was expired, and he barely looked like he was in his mid-twenties. The officer was going to take one look at that March 3, 1960, birthdate and laugh his ass off, and Diego wasn't in the mood to find out how brown men with fake IDs were currently being treated in the American Southwest.

"Maybe it'll turn out to be a good thing," Val said hopefully. "I don't know how yet, but..."

Diego snorted. "There's optimism, and then there's you," he teased lightly. "We could always try to find Tiffany, I guess. At Hellebore or something."

"I doubt Tiffany wants us showing up at Hellebore. Her brother might get suspicious, since he basically threw us out. And anyway, this is where we told the alpha to meet us, and we don't have any way to get in touch with him to change the location."

Diego hummed, folding his arms over the steering wheel and watching as teenagers and young adults kept turning up from who-knew-where, like scorpions popping up out of the sand and skittering across the busted pavement. This lot probably wouldn't be around much longer; Diego had a feeling that some parking deck company somewhere was drooling over this prime piece of real estate, only a few blocks from the Strip. Stabilize the foundation, build vertical, and start charging forty-five bucks a day. Bam. Instant profit.

A rap on the driver's side window startled him so badly he nearly jumped out of his skin, but when he looked up, it was to a smile he recognized under cotton-candy-blue bangs.

"Hey, new kid!" Rayne yelled through his window. "You come to play or what?"

"Friend of yours?" Val drawled from the passenger's seat as Diego lowered the window.

"Hey, what is this?" he asked. "Is this here all the time?"

"Nah. This is a Friday Fangers pop-up party. Never hits the same place twice." She leaned over and waved to Val. "You should both come. Vamps, humans, whatever. Somebody's sure to have goodies to share, though I can't vouch for the legality or integrity of any of them." She laughed. "Dealer will sell you a Snake Bite, come back twenty minutes later, buy another one, and find out he just sold you a Mothwing for the same price."

"I...have no idea what any of that is," Diego admitted.

"All the more reason to come play!" Rayne grinned and hopped two steps back from the door, eager and adorable. "Za's not here tonight. That's my girlfriend. You saw her at the Juice Bar. She said she had something for work she couldn't get out of. Can you imagine? Being immortal and still having a *job*?"

Rayne kept talking at a fast clip as Diego and Val reluctantly climbed out of the car to follow her, Diego making sure to lock it and set the alarm. He could do without some sky-high "fanger" deciding to take it for a joyride.

"There's been some trouble in the established clubs lately," Rayne was saying as they crunched across the pebbles and asphalt fragments in the parking lot. "Apparently some bigwig vampires have been squabbling?" She shrugged. "It doesn't really affect me that much yet, I guess, so I don't really pay attention to it. She works security, though, so no fun for her tonight. Atmosphere's *way* less tense at these things. Not so much annoying posturing."

"How long do these usually last?" Diego asked, shouting to be heard above the music as they got closer to the center, stepping around the scraggly daisies struggling up from the cracks in the asphalt.

Rayne shrugged. "Depends on how much fun everyone's having, and if someone does something stupid that gets the cops called on us." She rolled her eyes. "You'd think it would just be the teenagers, but it's mostly grown men harassing us. Some jerkwad brought a fucking attack dog to the last one. He ran away as soon as a couple of people started chasing him. I hope they caught him and kicked his ass."

Diego and Val stood close together as Rayne bounced off to talk to someone else she knew, and Diego couldn't help searching the faces in the crowd. Was Carlos here? Oddly, he thought he'd feel better if his cousin *was* here; that would at least mean he was in the scene and knew what he was doing and had just made a poor decision to go on a date with Vampire Dave. Diego didn't like thinking that Carlos had been... whatever the scientific term was for that weird brain-melty thing that happened when drowning in vampire pheromones. *Whammied*, maybe. If what Diego had felt was Val holding himself back, he could only imagine how overpowering it would be from a vampire who was using it on purpose.

"Do you think she knew about this?" Val asked, voice pitched low enough not to carry, but Diego heard him just fine. "Tiffany, I mean."

"Maybe, but I don't get why she would set us up to meet here in the middle of a flash mob."

"Unless she wanted backup. You heard what that girl said—people from this group chased off someone who brought an attack dog. She didn't even sound like it was that big of a deal. The werewolves wouldn't be able to safely shift surrounded by this many vampires and sympathizers."

Diego grunted, but he couldn't help thinking of how Apollo hadn't seemed willing to even entertain the idea that Tiffany's offer could be genuine. What if Apollo was right? What if vampires—not *all* vampires, obviously, but specifically *these* vampires, ancient Greek siblings who dispensed justice on their own whims and apparently had no qualms about betraying each other—did make promises just to break them?

His stomach sank. What if Tiffany had used him to lure the werewolf alpha out here without his pack? What if she wasn't planning an alliance, but an ambush?

"Godfuckingdammit," he muttered. "I'm such an idiot. It's a fucking trap."

She didn't care about stopping Vampire Dave. She'd said as much. She'd just used *their* need to stop him against them. And here they were, all of them, playing right into her hands. The only thing Diego could really hope for at this point was convincing her that he'd fulfilled his end of the bargain, so she was required to produce David or at least where to find him.

"Maybe...not," Val said weakly.

"I love that you actually said those words with your mouth," Diego muttered. "If I ever have to receive devastating news, I want you to be the one to deliver it to me."

"Ugh, I hope not."

Someone had brought dozens of folding camp chairs and set them up in one corner of the former lot, and someone else was trying to get a fire going in a trash barrel not far away. Because it wasn't like it could ever be too early to create a fire hazard. At least there was a grate over the top and there didn't seem to be anything particularly flammable around it.

The camp chairs were as good a place as any to keep watch, and whatever else they were, the so-called Friday Fangers were at least friendly. Diego lost count of the number of times someone offered him a drink, some food, or a joint—and for at least an hour there was practically a queue in front of Val, a constantly revolving line of people shyly offering him their wrists or necks or, in some bold cases, the artery on the inside of their thigh.

And no matter how hungry or thirsty Diego was, he kept turning down all offers of sustenance, because every time someone else held out their arm or hitched up their hem in front of Val, the only thing holding back Diego's incandescent rage was Val's unshakably polite disinterest. And if Val wasn't eating or drinking, well, Diego wasn't going to either. It was only fair.

If he bites anyone, it's damn well going to be me.

Diego was still simmering in his sullen frustration when he saw him: Carlos, looking lost and sad, wandering in vague circles. He didn't stop to talk to anyone, didn't take any of the offered food or soda or beer. He didn't appear to even hear the music from someone's bass-boosted Bluetooth speakers, but Diego couldn't tell from this distance whether Carlos had a mark on his neck. Had Vampire Dave bitten him? Had he ever been bitten before?

"What is it?" Val asked quietly, blatantly ignoring yet another supplicant. "I can feel how tense you are from six inches away."

Diego nodded toward Carlos, not wanting to be too obvious. "That's my cousin. The one who was with David at Roseblood."

Val looked where Diego indicated and gave a displeased noise. "He doesn't look like he's doing too well," Val admitted. "He looks like he's been glamoured. Pheromone hangover."

Glamoured, huh? Better than *whammied*, he guessed.

"I want to check on him," Diego admitted, "but my family can't know I'm here. Aside from the whole werewolf thing, they'd want to know why I can't come home yet." The word *home* almost didn't make it past the sudden tightness in his throat.

"Do you want me to talk to him?" Val asked hesitantly. "If he's still under the effect of the pheromones at all, I don't know how he'll react."

Maybe it was selfish, but Diego couldn't stand the thought of his cousin fawning over Val. He wasn't going to examine which part of the equation bothered him more, but he could tell himself it was for Carlos's sake.

"No, let's not take that chance," he said, shifting restlessly in the camp chair. Fuck. Maybe he'd try to get closer, to at least see if there were bite marks on Carlos's neck. If Vampire Dave really was the one Rayne had mentioned who only liked blood-virgins, maybe Carlos would be safe if David had already bitten him and then let him go.

"He never bites the same person twice," she'd told him. What a weird trait for someone who wanted to tie someone up in his basement to feed on them. Maybe it hadn't been Dave after all.

"If he's going to stick around the scene long," Val was saying to Diego in a transparent attempt to make him feel better, "he'll get a better handle on how to deal with the pheromones. They won't affect him as strongly, and he won't get the hangovers. Especially the more you're bitten by the same vampire, apparently, you develop a kind of immunity. Or so I've heard."

Diego blinked as the pieces started falling into place. "So, theoretically, if someone was choosing a particular victim and they wanted to...to glamour them, they would want someone who hadn't been bitten much? Or at all?"

"Theoretically," Val agreed casually, and Diego made a frustrated noise. It was proof of how many curious questions Val tolerated from him that the vampire didn't seem to think anything of the line of questioning now.

"So, *theoretically*," Diego emphasized, "if someone wanted to whammy someone long enough to tie them up in their basement and hook them up to a drip, they would pick someone without a lot of bite marks."

"Oh." Val looked back at Carlos. "You think he's the one Dave picked?"

"I don't know," Diego admitted. "Rayne had told me something about — Wait, Rayne!" He sat up quickly in the camp chair, twisting around to look for the blue-haired pixie. Maybe he couldn't let his cousin know he was in Vegas, and maybe it was too dangerous for a vampire to approach Carlos in his current state, but Rayne was a neutral third party and seemed like she was just naturally the helpful sort.

He had thought she'd be easier to spot, but strictly speaking, Diego hadn't been prepared for how many colorfully haired people there would be at a vampire-fucker pop-up party.

Diego leaned close to Val so he didn't have to shout. "Will you do me a favor? Can you keep an eye on where Carlos ends up? I'm going to go look for Rayne to see if she'll talk to him."

Val nodded. "Yes, of course. If I see her first, I'll let her know you're looking for her."

There were a few apparent vampires mixing with the other partygoers, but not as many as Diego would have guessed. Every single one of them bared their fangs at Diego as he passed but otherwise didn't attempt to interact with him, and he had no idea why until a familiar voice said from beside him, "You must smell particularly strange."

He looked over to see Rayne grinning at him. "Why do you say that?"

She laughed and pointed to one of the vampires who had curled their lip at Diego and then turned away. "They're like horses. Bare their teeth and back off if they don't like the smell of something."

Diego was a heartbeat from blurting out that Val always told him he smelled like werewolf before he remembered that this group of vampires didn't have even the tentative peace with their Lycan neighbors that Ashton and Pine Grove had managed to broker. In fact, they were somewhat actively at war, if Tiffany was to be believed.

"I swear I took a shower," he joked instead. "Anyway, I was looking for you."

Once he'd explained briefly, without getting into anything about Vampire Dave, Rayne agreed to check on Carlos for him and report back with her findings. While she approached Carlos, Diego returned to the pair of chairs where Val was still sitting.

"Well," Val said as he approached, "It's getting pretty late. I don't think they're coming. Once you find out about your cousin, if you want to go ahead and leave, we can get you home before—"

A commotion at one side of the parking lot drew their attention, the crowd of partygoers parting like a stage curtain as a dark-haired man in a striking white suit strode through, accompanied by four very intimidating-looking people, two on each side. Was one of them Rayne's girlfriend?

"Oh no." Val's little gasp caught Diego's ear.

"Oh no what?"

The white-clothed man drew himself up, and Diego felt as if all the air in Nevada was suddenly pressing in on his eardrums, the voice reverberating through him: "**Theophania.**"

From entirely too close for Diego's comfort—*Fuck, has she been here the whole time!?*—Tiffany answered, "Hello, brother. We've been waiting for you."

CHAPTER NINETEEN

"You said you had something for me," Jason said—because, Diego realized, that's who it was, Jason the Ancient Asshole Archon who had denied Val's request to stop Vampire Dave from ruining more people's lives. "I don't see anything here interesting enough to drag me out all this way."

"It's coming," Tiffany said loftily, motioning something forward. Two people in all black stepped forward, dragging a third person between them, and Val tensed as they threw Vampire Dave onto the pavement and stepped away. David groaned but didn't move. He was looking a little worse for the wear, Diego thought, but where was Carlos? Diego looked to the last place he'd seen his cousin, but although he spotted Rayne, Carlos was nowhere to be seen. Hopefully he was smart enough to leave.

Jason arched an imperious eyebrow, and Tiffany laughed. "Oh, no that one's not for you. That one's a payment I promised my little helpers." She looked straight at Diego and Val and then gestured to David. "All yours."

Shit. Well, at least she'd kept her end of the bargain, Diego thought wildly. But that must mean that the werewolves had shown up, and he hadn't seen or smelled them anywhere. He found out why when a white Escalade rolled onto the pavement and Tiffany's assistants opened the back door. Apollo strode out first, but Corbin was right behind him, both of them practically bristling.

"Ah, here's yours, brother." Tiffany crossed her arms, smiling. "I just thought, instead of all this sneaking around we've been doing, losing good people left and right, that it might be better for us to face each other out in the open for a fair fight." She chuckled. "Well. Maybe not *fair*. I haven't decided yet. But by my calculations, no matter which one of you survives this, I come out on top."

"Shit," Diego hissed. This was going to get messy, and Vampire Dave was *right there*—although he'd have to cross in front of the werewolves to get to him—but he also felt like he was responsible for Apollo and Corbin having shown up here. Apollo had been right, and Diego felt like an ass. He ought to stay and help them fight.

"I'm going to go get David."

It took a full five seconds for Diego to realize what Val had said, and by the time he did, Val was already up from his chair and walking toward David's prone body.

"Val!" Diego hissed. "What are you doing? I thought you didn't want him to know—"

Val paused, and Diego could see the determination in his eyes. "No. I don't really want him to know I'm here. But if he's allowed to keep doing whatever he wants, he's going to kill someone. Hurt someone. And it might be your cousin—or it might be someone else's cousin or sibling or child. And it would be my fault for letting him go."

"I thought you said the only way to kill a vampire was beheading or sunlight." Diego kept his voice as quiet as possible, not wanting to gain any unwanted attention for saying that out loud in present company. "It's not morning yet, and it's not like we're going to be able to just chop his head off out here in the parking lot."

"I'm not planning to kill him," Val mused. "I don't think. But murder and kidnapping are both human crimes as well. I'm going to turn him in."

Oh my God. That was the single worst plan Diego had ever heard of. Where was his evidence? Was he planning to tell the cops that *he* had been David's kidnapping victim in 1983 and hope they believed him?

A roar shook the air and Diego automatically ducked, realizing a moment later that it had come from Apollo. He was already well over six feet tall, but as Diego watched, he seemed to grow even taller, bulkier, with golden hair—no, fur—catching the low, shimmering lights. Oh. *Oh.* Diego had seen Haley do this exactly twice. She'd told him it was a special form of shapeshifting only alphas were taught. He'd thought Haley had looked huge when she'd done it—significantly taller than her usual five-four—but Apollo towered over everyone.

"Holy shit..." Maybe they didn't need Diego's help after all; it wasn't like he could shift into wolf form on command yet, like Corbin was doing at Apollo's side. He'd probably just get in the way.

What he could do, he figured, was go help Val drag that fucker Vampire Dave somewhere away from the terrifying, bloody fight that was about to go down and figure out what to do with him.

Except Dave was gone. Where—?

There. Fleeing down a nearby alley with Val on his heels but losing ground. Dammit, Val hadn't had enough to eat to be doing things like chasing people down alleyways.

With one last glance toward where Apollo was practically blocking out the Vegas skyline—he *really* did not need Diego's help—Diego turned and ran toward the mouth of the alley where Val and Dave had disappeared.

It smelled terrible, and he quickly realized why as he saw the line of dumpsters farther down the sidewalk. He could hear a scuffle, grunts and yelps and shuffling, and could just make out two men wrestling near one of the dumpsters. And then Val went toppling over backward, striking the pavement *hard*, and Diego lurched forward with a sharp cry.

He slid one hand under the back of Val's head, fingers threading through his hair, frantically feeling for any blood, while his other hand checked for any other injuries.

"I'm fine," Val protested with a wince, although when he tried to sit up, he couldn't quite make it. "I'm all right. Just...he's been live feeding, and he's stronger than me." He caught Diego's hand that was still patting over his torso, and Diego could feel in his grip just how weak he was.

"Listen. I'll be back on my feet in a minute. But David's getting away. You don't have time to wait for me."

Fuck! Diego looked down the alley where David had gone; if he hurried, he could probably track him.

"Okay." Diego carefully laid Val back down on the sidewalk. "I'll get him for you." Without conscious thought, he pressed a kiss to Val's forehead like he was sealing a promise, and then he tore down the alleyway.

David was nowhere to be seen, but there was a clatter and a shout across the street and down another alley, and Diego felt the wolf within him leap to the hunt.

The moon was so close to full, and his body was so close to changing, that he felt if he just stretched out on all fours, he could run faster, leap closer, catch his prey by the heel or the leg. His teeth felt sharp in his mouth, and he wanted to sink them into flesh—not just because the hunt sang in his blood, but because the coward fleeing from him needed to *pay* for what he'd done.

It took him longer than he would have liked to catch up, but finally David made a mistake and turned down a dead-end. Diego skidded to a stop, breathing hard, and they stared at each other, each silently daring the other to make the first move.

Diego felt the first wave like a punch between the eyes and shook his head. His eardrums popped from the pressure, and he gasped as he felt the weight of what could only be Dave attempting a pheromone whammy. *Glamour.* Whatever. Where Val's had felt seductive and intimate, had filled Diego with a hollow sense of longing, what he felt now was like being pulled under a heavy tide, unable to move and overcome with a dark need to sleep...and maybe never wake up.

He struggled against it, but he couldn't even lift his arms to push Dave away when he came closer, could only groan in protest when Dave tilted Diego's chin with cool, clammy fingers, exposing his throat.

You've got to be fucking kidding me, Diego thought through the haze. This fucker was going to try to bite him? Hell, no. *The only vamp that gets to bite me is in an alley two blocks that way.*

What had Val told him in Roseblood, how to resist the pheromones? Something about the eyes.

Dave's hand was sliding down his neck now, pushing aside the collar of his shirt and—

"What the fuck?" Dave pulled his hand away like he'd been burned, and Diego dimly realized he'd uncovered the gnarly scar from the werewolf bite. It wasn't much, but it broke Dave's concentration enough that Diego pushed back from him, breaking eye contact, bracing himself with one hand on the wall as he coughed and gasped for air as he regained control over his body.

As his senses slowly returned, Diego noticed the air around him becoming lighter, less dark. The walls of the alley were lit up in deep red and pink, orange creeping in at the edges as the sky overhead lightened to purple. Why was that important? Why did he need to get inside—?

"You little—" David took advantage of his weakness and shoved him up against the wall of the building, his head ringing as it bounced off the bricks. Nausea rose in his throat from the pain, and he crumpled to his knees as David stepped over him, scrambling toward the only exit, the way they'd come.

Fuck! He was getting away, and Diego could barely stand up.

He managed to stagger a few steps, clawing his way along the wall, but as he stumbled into the street beyond, the first rays of the morning sun crested the horizon—and kindled an explosion of flame.

CHAPTER TWENTY

DIEGO STUTTERED TO A STOP ON THE EDGE OF THE SIDEWALK, EYES wide at the bonfire rising in the middle of the street from the pile of ashes that used to be Vampire Dave. Aside from the few early-morning tourists and Strip employees headed home from work, the street was echoingly empty. No one seemed to think anything of the immolation that had just happened; probably thought it was a street performer. Diego probably wouldn't have given it a second glance if he'd been heading home from an overnight shift at the hotel, back in his former life, when werewolves were still just fiction, and when his head wasn't swimming with the mother of all hangovers from fucking vampire pheromones of all things.

Vampires.

Val!

The sun's sharp golden fingers were clawing their way up the pavement when Diego got back to where he'd left Val, weakened and hungry from too long without enough to eat. Had Val managed to get up? Had he moved, at least out of the way of the sun?

There—a pair of legs sticking out from between a dumpster and some very stinky trash bags.

"Val!" Fuck, oh fuck—would the sunlight hurt him if it just touched his pants legs and not his skin?

"Val, are you—" He bent over to try to check on the prone body but immediately gagged, close to retching, the overwhelming scent of trash rekindling the nausea from his hangover and maybe-concussion. "Oh—fuck," he gasped, trying desperately not to vomit. "Come on, let's get you...somewhere."

He couldn't even tell if Val could hear him, but he didn't have time to check. He held his breath as he slung Val's arms over his shoulders, dragging him away from the dumpster, farther down the alley and away from the creeping sunlight.

He was trembling with exhaustion by the time he got Val to the far side of the alley; at least the towering hotel across the street should shield them as the sun got higher. It could buy him a little time. He slumped against the wall and heaved Val into his lap. He laid his fingers against the side of Val's throat, panicking for a moment before he remembered that Val didn't have a heartbeat anyway—there was nothing to check for. He leaned over, putting his face close to Val's lips to try to detect if there was any movement of breath...

There. Just a little, a bare puff of air against his skin.

"You need to eat." He managed to lever Val into a mostly upright position, leaning against Diego's chest, his face slumped into the curve of Diego's neck. "C'mon, goddamn it," Diego panted, jostling him a little, like it might help.

Val groaned—faintly, but the noise was real, and Diego's pulse jumped. Desperately, one arm straining to keep Val upright, Diego grabbed the cuff of his other sleeve between his teeth and tugged. He got it halfway to his elbow—*Good enough.* The veins in his wrist thrummed close to the surface, purple cords under brown skin.

"Val," he said, struggling to find an angle where he could fit his wrist against Val's mouth. "I need you to wake up enough to eat. I need you to bite me, okay? Just this once."

Val's lips formed something that might have been "Okay," but his fangs remained withdrawn. The breath against Diego's skin was becoming fainter, with longer stretches between the exhales, and Diego clutched him tightly with both arms, fighting down panic and tears. Down the alleyway, the long fingers of the rising sun crept closer, and Diego stared helplessly. There was nowhere left to go. If Val couldn't bite him, couldn't feed, this was it.

Near the dumpster where he'd found Val, something glinted in the golden light: a bottle, broken into jagged pieces. They were lucky Val hadn't been lying on top of it and been sliced open. The vampire already had to supplement the blood in his body by ingesting it; he didn't need to lose any more.

Christ, he probably had shards of glass in his own shoes from standing over there.

Wait.

He probably had shards of glass in his shoes!

It took some delicate balancing to turn his leg where he could see the bottom of his shoe without dumping Val out of his lap, but once he did, he'd never been so glad to see a sharp, sparkling splinter inches from his skin. He managed to pick the little wedge out of the rubber sole, hissing when it pricked his fingertips.

"I swear to fuck, if I get tetanus because you wouldn't fucking bite me in the bathroom last night, I'm never speaking to you again," Diego muttered as he examined the point. It ought to be enough. He had to shift Val again to get at an angle where he could place the shard against his arm, and Val slid down his body, neck at an awkward angle braced against Diego's chest, but his hands were free.

He winced as he braced himself for the cut. "*Fuck!* Ow!"

It stung like hell, but it barely made a scratch, just little pinpricks of blood bubbling up to the surface of his skin, definitely not enough to feed a vampire, and it started slowing almost right away. It wasn't going to work. Diego dropped the glass shard and wrapped his arms around Val again as he smeared the precious little bit of blood across Val's lower lip.

"I'm sorry," he whispered. Sure, they'd neutralized the threat of Vampire Dave, but at what cost? He laid his hand against Val's cheek, skimming his hair back away from his face—and felt the moment when Val inhaled, sharp and sudden.

"You smell..." Val nosed against his neck, and an electric thrill shuddered through Diego. Something scraped lightly over his skin—were Val's fangs out?

"You're hungry, right?" Diego said, coaxing him. "Bite me."

Val groaned, and Diego couldn't tell if he was arguing or just miserable. Probably both.

The fangs pressed in a little more, a pinch of pain as the point scraped across the skin. Was he too weak to bite down or was he being stubborn? A warm drop slid down Diego's neck, then another, but Val didn't bite, and he wasn't drinking.

"Whatever personal preferences you may have, this time you have to swallow." Diego bit back a desperate laugh. "Ah, fuck. You better remember that when you're awake because it was fucking funny."

Val's tongue lapped gently against his skin, cleaning away the little trail of blood—and before Diego had time to do more than shiver, Val sealed his mouth over Diego's neck and the twin fangs sank deep.

The cry that burst out of Diego was equal parts surprise, pain, and —*oh God*, how did that feel good? He groaned, practically melting, and Val's arms twined around him, keeping him upright. Through the haze of euphoria, he realized Val's strength must be returning. *Oh good. It's working.*

Diego's body responded without his thought or consent. His fingers curled into the back of Val's shirt, his back arching as an ache of arousal settled between his legs, low and deep and craving.

Val clutched him tightly, tongue lapping against Diego's feverish skin. The fangs had withdrawn, but the blood was still flowing, almost as if it would rather be in Val's mouth than in Diego's veins. Diego couldn't blame it.

Was it pheromones working him up like this? He was pretty sure being bitten by a werewolf hadn't included any elements of pleasure, just pain and fear. And maybe it wouldn't feel this good if it was someone who didn't care about him at all, but at the moment the clearest thought in his head was, *No wonder Rayne has a tattoo about this.*

Val tore himself away suddenly, specks of blood spattering over his chin, and Diego arched up sharply with a groan. Val pressed the back of his wrist to his mouth, swallowing thickly and loudly.

Christ, Diego felt like he'd orgasmed, but there was no physical evidence that he had.

"Feel better?" Diego rasped, and Val nodded silently, worrying at his lower lip. "You can't possibly feel as good as I do." Diego chuckled and reached up to press one fingertip against the sharp edge of Val's still-extended fangs. He probably shouldn't think they were beautiful, but he did.

"I'm sorry," Val said quietly. "Sorry I...had to bite you." He shuddered. "I'm sorry I didn't stop sooner. I was...I was hungry, and it was hard—"

"I'm sorry I had to make you bite me," Diego said, finally struggling to a sitting position of his own. "And honestly, I'm sorry you had to stop at all, because speaking of hard..."

He grinned over at Val—and immediately realized something was very, very wrong. Little pinpricks of rapidly darkening pink were springing up all over Val's face and arms, almost like...

"Oh shit—you're blistering! We have to get you out of the sun."

His stomach lurched; he'd just seen one vampire immolated in direct sunlight. How was he going to get Val out of this alleyway without exposing him?

"We have to get you home," Val added, pulling his arms inside his shirt sleeves. Did that help? Was there a blanket or a jacket or...anything? Diego ripped his own shirt off, draping it over Val's head like a veil.

"The car's a long way from here." Diego looked around frantically. "And I don't think we can stay in the shade the whole time."

The scuffing of shoes along the asphalt caught his ear and he whirled, instinctively putting his body between Val and the person approaching them. Silhouetted against the pale morning, a hazy halo behind his towering form, Apollo lived up to his divine namesake. Diego was more relieved than he'd expected that his side—did these werewolves count as *his* side?—had apparently won the showdown.

And then Apollo opened his mouth. "I warned you that if you weren't gone by nightfall, I was going to report you to the regional authority."

"Oh come the fuck on, man," Diego groaned. "Really?"

"But..." Apollo continued, holding up one finger, "my husband has talked me out of it this one time, considering the extenuating circumstances. So as long as you promise not to trespass here again, I'm going to pretend I never saw you."

"Good. You can fuck right off while you're at it," Diego huffed.

Apollo tilted his head. "Sure, I can do that, if you'd rather *not* have help getting back to your car safely," he said, and Diego eyed him suspiciously. "After all, the full moon is tonight, and I have a feeling you're expected elsewhere."

CHAPTER TWENTY-ONE

LELAND HAD SHUFFLED OUT OF HER BEDROOM A LITTLE AFTER TWO IN the afternoon looking like death warmed over and declared that he was fine. Haley hadn't believed him then, and as she intentionally slowed her steps so as not to leave him behind on the bustling sidewalk, she believed him even less now.

"I know you wanted to be part of Halloween," she said gently as she twined their fingers together—mostly to try to keep him steady as wide-eyed tourists kept brushing and bumping into them on all sides. "But I think we might just have to let you sleep through it and plan to try again next year."

Wait—did that kid have a caramel apple and a bag of candy corn? She peered a bit closer and couldn't help laughing. The bag of candy had the Carmody Bed & Breakfast logo on the side. Dang, but Brooks knew how to hustle. The apple at least was probably handmade from scratch. Brooks made divine caramel.

Leland made a disgruntled noise beside her, catching her attention again. "I can still help," he insisted hoarsely. "Just because I'm not on duty tonight doesn't mean I'm useless."

Haley bit back a sigh and tried very, very hard not to let the frustration show in her face. He'd been so darn stubborn ever since he'd started feeling unwell—and she knew something about being stubborn, but she also felt like she knew when to admit defeat and take a sick day.

But she had a feeling it had something to do with the parents he never talked about. The fact that he never mentioned them, not even in passing, had already piqued her suspicion, but when she'd talked to his little sister the other day, a lot of pieces had fallen into place.

The girl had been so apologetic and painfully polite from the moment Haley had answered the phone.

"I don't mean to bother you, and I'm sorry for speaking so quietly. My father is asleep and..."

And maybe that wouldn't have sounded quite the way it did if Haley didn't know that Leland never mentioned their dad but spent a lot of time and energy trying to take care of his baby sister from the next state over.

"It's okay to not be useful sometimes, you know," she said gently, but a shout from across the street got Leland's attention. She craned her neck to see where he was looking and sighed as she recognized the other two Upham County deputies, reflective vests hanging open over their coats.

"Hey, Sommers!" One of them—if she was honest, she never could remember which was which—waved as they both headed across the street. Leland stepped away from her, and it took a minute to realize he was trying to get her to let go of his hand.

Well, all right then. She dropped his hand and crossed her arms. If that's the way they were playing it.

"We thought we'd come on down and enjoy some of it before the real fun starts," the shorter one said. She decided he'd be Walker, if only to keep them straight in her head. "Moonrise is about eight o'clock tonight, so I figure we got a couple of hours before we really gotta start worrying about anything. Guess I should find the preserve lady and ask for sure, though, see what her plans are for the tours tonight."

Leland grunted. "You mean *this* preserve lady?" he drawled, pointing his thumb at Haley.

Walker seemed to notice her for the first time. "Oh, I thought— Did it used to be someone else? Kinda looked like you though?"

"It was my mother," Haley said. "I took over last year, but we didn't do the public run."

Walker snapped his fingers. "That's right! I remember you bein' a lot smaller though. Guess it's been a while since we saw you. Anyway, we're on traffic duty tonight, but if you have any trouble with those Meagher County boys, you come talk to us."

"I'll do that," Haley said, amused. "I think Karen Fenton, the veterinarian, is the person you'll want to talk to if you want information about the tour. I'll be out on the preserve tonight."

It wasn't even a lie. She'd be on the preserve all night actually, until the sun came up the next day. She glanced over at Leland. Maybe she should set him up at the ranger's cabin where the pack would be. But then what if he needed something? Anyone nearby would be a wolf, and he'd be a long, long walk from town.

"Listen, Sommers—" Donaldson this time. Or the taller one, at least. "I know you're off duty tonight, but do you have the keys to the office on you? Be a good place to stash our stuff. The Meagher boys too. We'd usually just leave it in the truck, but that feels like askin' for trouble with this many people."

"Yeah," Walker put in. "Few years ago, Donaldson left the keys in the truck, and some teenager took it joyriding straight into a pond."

Leland gave her a sidelong look, and she laughed genuinely, holding up both hands. "Not me, that time." It did sound like something she would've done, but not on Halloween.

"I've got the keys," Leland finally said, like he'd been debating whether to admit it.

"Great! You can walk over with us and let us in."

She watched him fidget, cornered, then finally nod.

"I'll catch up with you," Haley assured him. "I need to go check on a couple of things."

She deliberately didn't kiss him goodbye, since it seemed like he didn't want his coworkers to know anything was going on between them. Probably for the best; it might not be the most professional look in the world. Hadn't she been in the same predicament with her pack just a few months ago?

Halfway across the street, though, her werewolf-sharp hearing picked out Walker saying, "Hey, she's not half-bad, right? You ever think about hitting that?" and then a quick, nervous follow-up: "I didn't mean anything by it! Just runnin' off at the mouth. You know me."

She chuckled. She'd have to tease Leland about that later, when he was feeling better—which she fiercely hoped was soon, and not just for his sake. Once the full moon was past, she wouldn't feel *quite* so much like she was going to crawl out of her skin, but she only had so much self-control and she'd used pretty much all of it this week. As soon as he was *actually* on the mend instead of tottering around like a flu-zombie, all bets were off.

Walker and Donaldson at least were normal levels of annoying. The five "loaners" from Meagher County seemed polite enough when they also stored their jackets and lunchboxes and personal effects behind Leland's battered desk, but he still would've felt better if he was going to be personally keeping an eye on them.

Maybe he could. Haley would be out on the preserve before eight o'clock. Maybe he could just head back downtown in an unofficial capacity. Just to keep an eye on things. Sure, he still felt like he'd been chewed up and spit out, and walking anywhere right now sounded like a terrible idea, but he had a couple of hours to take a nap before he had to worry about that.

"You know," mused one of the officers he didn't know, a tall man with dark skin and an attractively deep voice, "my granddad swears up and down there really are werewolves in this town. Or at least there used to be." He chuckled, and the rest of the officers joined in with him. "He claims to have seen one of them a couple dozen years ago, wouldn't listen to a word I said when I tried to explain that all kinds of animals live out here, and he probably just saw a regular wolf or a bear."

"There's a couple of those old codgers who seem to really believe it," one of his coworkers said. "Keep your eyes out tonight. Sometimes one or two of 'em will get a wild hair and try to do something—like the year

Mick Jansson decided he was going to smoke the whole pack out. Still have no idea where he got that many smoke bombs, but he said he uses 'em for squirrel hunting."

They kept chatting as they filed out of the office, Leland locking the door behind them. Against his better judgment, he took the office key off the ring and held it out to Donaldson. He still might not like the man, but he'd been decent enough about carting Leland around with a head injury.

"In case I'm still asleep at sunup when you all want to leave," Leland said, and Donaldson took it with a nod.

"Appreciate it. You get some rest. Rylan's finally feeling better after a week of being a walking plague vector, so you should be coming out of it any day now."

That was a comforting thought, but apparently that same evening didn't count as "any day now." He still felt like he was going to fall over any minute—and that would serve him right, seeing as he'd promised Haley and her mom that he'd stay home.

And he definitely should've still been asleep under that yellow quilt that smelled so much like Haley's shampoo, not walking the three quarters of a mile from Haley's house into the collection of five little businesses that counted as "downtown" for Pine Grove.

All five of them were lit up and overrun with people tonight. Benny's was cranking out pizzas as fast as their oven could bake them, and even the boot shop was doing a brisk business in souvenirs and belt buckles. He wasn't sure he'd been around this many people at once since he'd left Tucson.

His stomach churned at the thought, and he remembered Guerrera's text: *Niles is missing. Keep your eyes open.*

But he was two days' drive from Tucson. His case against Niles hadn't gone anywhere. There was no reason for Niles to come after him. No way he even knew where Leland was.

Right?

Pieces of conversation washed over him as the crowd parted around him as easily as if he were a badly placed streetlamp.

A pair of young women: "You really think there'll be anything to see?"

"I heard there's actually wolves out there. I guess they probably use a drone or something to herd them up where we can hear them."

"That makes sense..."

What looked like maybe a dad and his teenage son: "Can't believe there's still places where things like this are free."

"Oh, they're making plenty of money. That boot shop's almost out of stock."

And then: "Got me some traps set right inside the edge of the preserve. Couldn't get farther in than that. Figure I'll head back out in the morning and see what's caught in 'em. Be funny as hell if it was a werewolf."

Leland looked around, but he couldn't see who'd said it. It hadn't sounded like Jacob Niles, surely. That had just been his imagination. There were five or six men nearby who looked likely to have said that, and a few more who didn't, and there was no way to tell which of them was bragging about having set wolf traps illegally in a nature preserve. He didn't see any of the officers either—Walker and Donaldson were down in the field that was serving as a makeshift parking lot, and none of the Meagher County loaners were visible from where he was.

He had to get word to Haley. He had to warn her.

He turned in a circle, getting his bearings slowly, until he was facing the direction of the nature preserve.

And then he started walking.

CHAPTER TWENTY-TWO

IT STARTED SNOWING NEAR THE IDAHO-MONTANA STATE LINE, JUST past the turnoff for Yellowstone, and Diego had never in his life been so happy to see thick, stubborn clouds covering the entire sky. They had a little over three hours to go until they hit Pine Grove, and just about that much time until the moon would rise. There was only so fast he could take the curvier parts of the road, especially if the snow started sticking, so he wasn't optimistic about shaving off much of that time.

He pulled over in the shadow of some fat, young pine trees and threw the car into park, running back to the trunk to open it and praying no one drove past for at least a few minutes.

"Val—"

The blanket Apollo had given them in Las Vegas to get them to the car safely was tucked around him as Val squinted up at Diego, still drowsy.

"Are we there? It feels early."

"No, we have a while to go." Diego looked up at the sky, blinking at the snowflakes that settled on his eyelashes. "It's still kind of light out, but there are clouds everywhere. No sun. I know it's a risk, but...can you come sit up front? I...I don't know if we're going to make it, and I need you to be able to take the wheel so I don't kill us both if I turn into a wolf."

Val sat up, nodding, catching the blanket around his shoulders like a cape. "I'll come. Do you want me to go ahead and drive?"

Diego shook his head. "No, I—need something to focus on." Something other than the fact that the moon was on its way and there wasn't a damn thing he could do to stop the change that would happen.

Getting Val out of the trunk was more awkward than getting him in, and Diego caught him by the elbows and then by the waist to steady him as he stepped out onto the pavement. They stood perfectly still, watching each other's eyes, Diego's pulse pounding in his throat. The little bite marks from that dirty, glowing alley in Vegas stung, just a little, just enough to remind him they were there. Val's tongue darted out over his lower lip nervously as a flurry of snow swirled between them, and Diego felt himself leaning forward before he could think twice.

"Di..." Val's breath, shaky and uncertain, skated across his lips, and Diego winced.

"You're right. We don't have time." They had *negative* time actually, and everything they'd been worried about the night before was still there. Diego stepped back and closed the trunk firmly. "We can...talk about it later." *If you're still speaking to me later.*

"I was just going to say," Val said, catching Diego by the elbow before he could walk back to the front of the car, "that I think you ought to let me drive. Your eyes are bloodshot. You've barely had any sleep at all since before we went to Roseblood."

"I..." Diego frowned. "Are you sure you can get us there in time?"

"No," Val said bluntly. "But can you?"

Diego stared down the road instead of meeting Val's gaze. He'd already known he likely couldn't make it to Pine Grove in time. Wasn't that why he'd dragged Val out of the trunk in the first place, even though it wasn't yet nightfall?

"Let me." Val reached up, and Diego held his breath as Val's fingertips hovered just above the side of his neck, almost touching the scabbed-over bite marks. "Please, Diego. Let me...take care of you."

The simple words in Val's soft, earnest voice tugged at some thread inside him, and he felt himself start to unravel. He turned back, bracing himself against Val's pleading look, and wet his lips.

"Okay." His voice was hoarse, almost unrecognizable to his own ears, but Val's whole face softened with relief. The hand hovering over his neck fell away without ever touching him, but Diego's skin burned like it was on fire.

By the time Diego made it to the passenger's side door, Val was already adjusting the mirrors and angle of the driver's seat.

"What, exactly, is the deadline?" Val asked as he clicked his seatbelt into place. "Is it when the moon is over where the horizon would be if it was flat? What if there's a mountain in the way? Is it when the moonlight touches you? What if the clouds are still there?"

"I don't know," Diego admitted. He leaned his temple against the cool glass of the window as Val steered the car back onto the road, gravel spitting up from the tires. "I know the clouds don't matter."

"Well, there goes that idea."

Diego had honestly thought he was too tightly wound to sleep, but he drifted into fitful, restless dreams before the next mile marker was past. Sorting out the images was next to impossible, tumbling over each other in his mind:

Making it back down the alley too late and finding ashes where Val had been.

The two of them seated at the table in Roseblood and everyone watching as Val drank deeply from him, Diego's own food neglected on the golden plate in front of him.

Hearing from his mother that his only cousin on his father's side had disappeared and they'd found his body weeks later, completely drained of blood.

The bathroom of the motel room at the Blooming Sagebrush, Val's body tangled with his as they ground against each other and traded breathless, groaning kisses until the alarm started going off in the other room.

He woke from the last one with a strangled gasp, then collapsed back against the seat as he realized they had all been dreams. Except the alarm, which had apparently been his subconscious's way of interpreting Val's phone beeping. Val, however, didn't seem to notice.

"Somebody texting you?"

"Hm? Oh. It's..." Val sighed. "David texted me a few weeks ago to... taunt me. It's how I knew where he was."

Oh. The *Happy anniversary, babe!* text. Damn.

"Anyway, for whatever reason, it keeps popping back up. I don't know if he set it to send multiple times or what. It was just once or twice a day, but it's coming in every few minutes now. Maybe it will stop after tonight, since it's Halloween."

"He..." Diego frowned, wetting his lips nervously. "I'm not sure if you were conscious enough to know what happened, but he's...dead."

"Oh." Val glanced away from the road for just a moment, just long enough to get his hand on his phone. When it pinged again, he turned the volume down. "I wondered."

"Sunlight," Diego said softly. "I didn't... He ran out into it."

He still wasn't sure if that counted as his fault. He'd been chasing the man; was he responsible? He sincerely hoped being a werewolf got slightly less murdery as time went on. At least his cousin wasn't tied up in Vampire Dave's basement though. He'd never have to *actually* get that phone call from his mother, and he considered the faint mark on his conscience a fair price to pay.

Val took a deep breath and let it out slowly, and Diego warmed with fondness at the deliberate exercise of it. After the last few days with other vampires who only used breath to speak, Val's habit of using it to regulate his emotions was...endearing.

"I feel a little bad for being relieved he's dead," Val finally admitted quietly, and Diego shook his head.

"No, that's not—" A ripple of *something* through Diego's body choked off his voice, his muscles tightening and then releasing, and then again. Oh fuck. He looked at the sky and cursed the fact that he could only tell it was getting dark, not where the moon was. They had almost an hour left to get back to Pine Grove, according to the GPS. He didn't have time for this.

"Di, are you all right?" Val's voice broke through his haze, but he didn't know how to answer. Was he all right? Or—

Another convulsion racked him; the car swerved, and he was dimly aware of Val reaching for him across the space between them.

"I'm all right," Diego panted, although he wasn't sure it was the truth. "Keep driving. Don't worry about me."

Diego was dimly aware of the car lurching up to a higher speed, of Val darting anxious glances at him, but all his concentration was on keeping his body human for as long as he could.

For the first time, he could see how the shift between human and wolf could eventually become voluntary. Up until now, he'd had no control over it whatsoever, but now he could sense where his will was tied up with the change, and he exerted every ounce of himself into *not* changing—not all the way, not yet.

Val kept darting worried glances at him from the driver's seat, but Diego couldn't spare the breath or energy to reassure him. Val wasn't driving nearly as fast as he had been, but he hoped Pine Grove was closer than it felt. Maybe he could stay in charge of himself enough *not* to be an instinct-ruled wild animal for a few minutes, even if he did change. Maybe he could keep the wolf from panicking and attacking Val.

"Just a little while longer," Val murmured, and Diego couldn't tell if he was trying to soothe the wolf or himself. But eventually it didn't matter—Diego could fight all he wanted, but even with the cloud cover, even with the mountains, the moon was up. Time had run out.

He felt his consciousness slip into a deep haze, the wolf bursting to the surface as his body finished the change. But for once, he wasn't completely helpless. It felt like trying to move through molasses or trying to control a dream, but if he tried hard enough, his transformed body would respond—at least enough that he didn't lunge at Val, didn't growl or snarl or snap. He didn't even particularly want to, which was both a surprise and a relief.

But it was exhausting, like swimming against a current, and finally he had to let go of any control and let the wolf be an anxious, whimpering mess, clawing at the door and window, too big for the small space.

He was distantly aware of the car stopping, of the car door opening, of his big, clumsy, wolfy body tumbling out onto the grassy shoulder beside a crumpled guardrail that felt oddly familiar.

"Go that way," Val said, pointing toward the trees that stood just past a flat field. "That's the preserve. The rest of the pack should be there. You'll be safe."

As if on cue, a ghostly howl floated up into the night, and an answer burst out of the wolf's throat and chest as he leaped forward.

CHAPTER TWENTY-THREE

THE FOREST WAS BREATHING. NO—THAT WAS THE WIND, LIFTING HIS hair and cooling the sweat that had gathered on his forehead. A distant howl shivered through the night, several others rising around it as the dark clouds broke for a moment, their edges dragging long, crooked fingers over the face of the moon and flurries of snow swirling down through the evergreens. A twig snapped behind him; he jumped and turned, flames flickering in his mind's eye. But there was no one there, no flexing werewolf extremist with a discount tiki torch, and no uniformed officer laughing as he let a snarling canine froth and flail at the end of its leash.

Why was he out here? God. It was hard to think past the hot, heavy pressure behind his eyes. He'd been tired before he started walking, and now his legs felt like they were about to fall off. He'd come for a reason. Someone needed him. Prudence? No. She was in Spirit Lake. *Haley*. But that didn't seem right. Haley didn't need his help.

"Got me some traps set right on the edge of the preserve."

Right. That was it. Haley didn't know about the traps. And he'd—what, come out here to tell her? Great idea, Sommers. *The fever's fried your brain.*

He remembered enough now, with another gust of the breeze washing over him, cooling him, to know it had seemed like his only choice at the time. And maybe it had been, but it was a shitty choice. Like joining the Tucson PD because it had been the highest-paying job he could get without a college degree.

Was that howl closer? There were more wolves out here than Haley and her pack. Would the American gray wolf pack that lived on the preserve be aggressive if he was in their territory? Damn. He should've brought a firearm. Why hadn't he?

"Wish you could shoot me, don't you, Sommers?" the shadow of Jacob Niles taunted him from the darkness between the trees.

Yeah. And maybe some part of him still wished he had. The stitches Leland had gotten in his arm were nothing compared to the horrified noises of the boys Leland had been standing in front of. Niles had thought it was funny that the kids were afraid of his canine partner and had urged the dog to lunge and bark at them.

Leland had stepped between the dog and the boys.

"Cut it out. Calm her down."

"Oh, get over yourself, Sommers. It's just like you not to be able to take a joke. She's on her leash."

Jake Niles hadn't liked him since Leland's first month on the force, when he'd blown the whistle on Niles's partner for punching a handcuffed suspect. There had been bodycam footage—Leland's—and witnesses to the incident, and Niles had a new partner within a matter of months. Leland didn't know exactly what had gone down with the other one. That had been a year before, but apparently Niles could hold a grudge.

"Just pull her in and let them pass. They're not hurting anybody."

The leash had slipped—deliberately. The dog had rushed forward another foot. One of the boys had started crying. Niles had laughed. Then, never breaking eye contact with Leland, he'd reached down and released the clasp.

Now, Leland stared at the flickering vision of Jake Niles in the snow, and he finally admitted it out loud. "Yeah, I do wish I could've shot you."

Niles grinned, canines looking especially sharp, and walked backward into the forest. *"Come on then. Come get me."*

Where was Diego? About an hour before the moon had come up, Haley had looked around the ranger's cabin at her pack and realized that he wasn't there. Between spikes of panic, she'd felt incredibly guilty that she hadn't thought of it before. Sure, there had been a lot going on, and sure, she wanted to show him she trusted him, but also, he *needed* to be with the pack when he changed, at least for the next few months. He needed older, more experienced wolves that could protect him while he was still getting used to it.

She'd texted him, tried calling him, but all she'd been able to do was leave him increasingly anxious voicemails. There wasn't enough time to drive up to Ashton looking for him and then get them both back before they turned, but maybe—maybe she could go looking for him anyway. At least if she was with him, he wouldn't be alone. That would leave the pack on their own, and the tourists without an alpha, but she owed it to Diego. He was part of her pack, and it was her job to take care of him.

"Mom," she called across the cabin. Already some of the pack members had undressed and run outside. One or two of them had shifted ahead of time and were roughhousing, playful growls and noises rising into the snowy night on clouds of their breath. She could feel the moon pulling at her too, but she still had a few minutes—she hoped. "Mom, I need your help."

Kimberly paused where she'd been folding her jacket over the back of a chair. "What is it? What do you need?"

"I need you to lead the run tonight." When Kimberly frowned, Haley rushed to get the rest out while she could still form words. "One of my pack is missing. I have to go look for him. But the run—"

"I understand." Kimberly hugged her tight. "I'll lead the run one more time. You go find your wayward pup."

Haley couldn't get undressed fast enough, leaving her clothes in a hasty pile as she flung herself into the transformation at record speed. The wolves who were already playing in the snow watched her with their heads cocked to the side, ears up curiously, as she tore past them, but she didn't have time to stop and explain things. She'd have to trust her mother to do that. She turned west, toward Ashton, and ran.

CHAPTER TWENTY-FOUR

THE FIRST TRAP TO BREAK THE NIGHT BETWEEN ITS METAL JAWS sounded like a gunshot, and Diego leaped straight into the air, barely pulling his paw back in time. He came down in the thick leaves on all fours only to hear the rapid-fire succession of the rest of the chain of traps as they set each other off. He yelped and bolted forward, deeper into the forest, something in the wolf remembering the other five times they'd run through these trees, even if Diego himself hadn't been awake for any of it.

He keenly felt the absence of the pack, though, and the safety it offered—the guidance of the other wolves, their guardianship. He missed them almost like he missed his family; the night felt vast and empty, and he lifted his nose into the night wind and howled with the ache of sudden loneliness.

An answering howl from close by caught his ear, and he leaped toward the noise, pausing when a distant echo sounded from the opposite direction. The wolf shivered in memory of being caught between two hunting packs the night its existence had been forced onto Diego, its first transformation in a spring storm.

He remembered, dimly, a man and a woman standing over him,

arguing over whether to kill him or let the wolf be created. The man had wanted to kill him. He'd tried, and the wolf had barely escaped.

A twig snapped to his right, and a bulky man-shaped shadow staggered out of the trees toward him. The hackles went up on the back of his neck, and he snarled. Not again! Not this time! This time he had teeth, and he was going to fight back.

Leland knew, somewhere deep inside, that the shadow of Jacob Niles he was following was entirely in his head. It wasn't real; he was just compelled to follow it. Maybe, he thought, his subconscious was leading him out of the preserve, since he was entirely lost.

Hell, for all he knew he was wandering in circles. Maybe he ought to start breaking the ends of some of the branches he was walking past so he could tell if he'd already been this way before.

The first one he snapped was louder than he expected, and he jumped, but the next few were easier. The third tree was dead, and the whole branch broke off in his hand, throwing him off-balance. He steadied himself, then froze as he heard the distinct sound of an angry, snarling dog.

No. He's not really here. He can't be. I'm just imagining things.

But whether Jake Niles was a phantom or flesh, the animal that leaped at him out of the darkness was very, very real, and so was the ghostly howl behind him.

Haley had heard a second wolf. The pack, she knew, was back closer to town, and she could hear them baying and calling back and forth—but there had been another voice, a lone wolf, closer to her. It had sounded like Diego's howl, and she wondered if he'd made it down from Ashton just in time after all.

He'd stopped responding to her a minute ago, though, and she worried what that meant. She wasn't as familiar with this side of the preserve; they didn't often come out this far during the runs, and even with the wolf's improved night vision, it was hard to see with the cloud cover as thick and dark as it was.

She howled again as she ran toward the last direction she'd heard maybe-Diego answer from, then slowed as she heard the snarling growl of a wolf that was past giving a warning. She lifted her nose to scent the wind, caught Diego's scent, and—what on *earth* was Leland Sommers doing out here?

A burst of speed brought her into the clearing just in time to see Diego rush forward toward Leland who was wielding what looked like an entire tree branch, and she did the only thing she could think to do. She launched herself between them.

There were *two* of them now? Leland staggered back as a second dog—no, this was bigger than a dog. *It's a wolf. They're both wolves.* His hands shook, and he gripped the tree branch harder. He hadn't had a weapon the first time, nothing except his body to put between an attacking German shepherd and a handful of middle school boys, and he'd paid for it in flesh and blood and eleven stitches. This time he wasn't letting go of the one defense he had.

He raised the branch over his head to strike them and then—froze. The second wolf was...protecting him? It was keeping the first one from lunging at him, blocking it every time it tried, but not fighting it. Leland lowered the branch slowly, cautiously, ready to raise it again if needed.

It wasn't needed. As he watched, the second wolf managed to calm the first one...and then it lay down on the ground and lowered its head between its paws, looking up at Leland calmly. The first wolf, the darker one, paced back and forth nearby, whining anxiously, coming closer to the bigger, lighter wolf, then looking up at Leland and dancing away.

Finally, finally it sank in. The big, light-colored wolf—he'd seen her before. Only a few times, but... "Haley?" She picked her head up, mouth curving up in a wolfy smile, and he threw the branch aside.

When he crouched down close and held one hand out, close but not touching, she butted her head up into his palm, and whatever shadows of the past had been haunting him in those woods faded away. Eventually, the other wolf mimicked her, lying down close to her, though it still eyed Leland somewhat distrustfully.

Once they'd all calmed down, Haley got up and loped away, then paused and turned back to them. She might not have been able to speak, but Leland knew a *Come on! Let's go!* when he saw one. He and the smaller wolf—if he had to hazard a guess, Diego, judging by the sparkling diamond still in its ear—followed behind her like a lopsided, obedient pack as she led them back out of the woods.

CHAPTER TWENTY-FIVE

Diego opened his eyes to sunlight, bright and blinding, and nearly burst out of his skin with panicked adrenaline. *Val!* He bolted upright in bed, and only when the blanket slid down his bare chest did he begin to register where he was.

He wasn't in the motel room. Val was not anywhere nearby; the midmorning sun was not a danger. It took an embarrassingly long time for anything else to filter through: The wood paneling on the walls, the sound of murmuring voices in the next room, the mouthwatering smell of bacon and cinnamon and coffee.

He was in the pack cabin on the preserve. And if his nose wasn't lying to him, someone was cooking breakfast.

Beside the bed where he'd woken up was a rustic table, and on it were his cell phone, his wallet, and a small box in metallic gift wrap and a golden bow, all set on top of his neatly folded shirt and pants. They were the ones he'd been wearing when they left Vegas, and there was at least one visible grass stain on the pants. He didn't even remember taking them off; Val must have gotten the wolf out of them at some point.

Which meant Val had dropped all this off for him. Including, maybe, the little gift box.

His stomach growled loudly, reminding him that he'd barely eaten on top of the metabolic drain that was the full-moon shift. Maybe he'd get food first so he could properly appreciate whatever was in that box—and to give himself time to prepare for whatever it was. Or wasn't.

He dressed, despite the uncomfortable feeling of putting on clothes that could really stand to be washed, and cautiously pushed open the wooden door. There were just a few people in the room, two or three he sort of knew from other runs, plus Haley, Brooks, Jo, and a blonde white woman he didn't recognize but who looked enough like Haley that he could begin to guess.

"Good morning," Brooks said with a warm smile, the first to hear him, and Haley whirled from where she was pouring herself a cup of coffee.

"You're up!" She grinned at him over the mug. "The town is still full of tourists, so we came prepared to have pack breakfast at the cabin instead of the diner. Brooks made a—what did you call it?"

"*Pain perdu*," Brooks said in a silky French accent, and Haley gestured.

"A pan peardoo," she imitated, to Diego's amusement. "Anyway, it looks like a French toast casserole to me, and it's delicious. He's got cinnamon apples and caramel to put on top if you want. And of course there's bacon and coffee."

"That...sounds amazing," Diego admitted as Haley handed him a plate and a fork. After he'd eaten and met the blonde woman—Haley's mother, as he'd predicted—his mind turned to that little silver box. He was dying to know what was in it, but he wanted to open it when he was alone. Just in case.

"Let me know when you're ready to go," Haley told him. "Michele should be back from her uncle's either tonight or tomorrow, so if you want you can stay..." She hesitated. "Uh, well, you can stay with me, but Leland and Mom are also currently staying with me, so we're short on sleeping space. The couch is free though."

"You can stay at the bed and breakfast," Brooks said easily, waving one hand. "I've been wanting to talk to you anyway. With the babies, we need an extra hand at the reception desk, and I heard that you have experience with that sort of thing. We can chat after you get settled in."

As far as he knew, Diego hadn't told Haley about his background in hospitality. Maybe he'd told Michele, or maybe... No. The vampires and werewolves still weren't officially on speaking terms. Even if Val had dropped off his things, there was no reason he would have made enough conversation with Brooks to get around to an employment reference. Maybe he'd ask about it next time they saw each other. Assuming Val still wanted to see him.

"Oh. Um. Sure. Just let me get my things."

He checked his phone as he tucked it into his pocket and had to admit he was disappointed there wasn't a message from Val waiting there. There were several from Haley, including a few voicemails, from the night before. Judging from the escalating anxiety in each text, she'd been worried sick about him, which—aside from the guilt that induced—was kind of heartwarming.

The little box he slipped into his pocket, where he could feel it practically burning through to his thigh the entire ride to the Carmody Bed & Breakfast.

"Of course you could've taken care of yourself at Michele's until she got back," Brooks was saying easily as he pulled into the parking area. "But I always appreciate some company after a full moon, so I thought you might too."

It didn't take Brooks long to get Diego set up in a smallish room on the top floor of the B&B. ("Sorry for the tiny space. The guest rooms are all full of...well, guests. We usually use this as a library.") And once the door was closed, Diego could finally breathe.

He sat down cross-legged in the center of the twin bed, shifting uncomfortably when the bed springs creaked beneath him, and set the box in his lap, gently tugging at the ribbon.

Inside the box were two square-cut emerald earrings, smaller than the diamond one he usually wore, but vivid and beautiful. As he plucked one of them out of the cushion, his phone vibrated three times in quick succession.

Texts.

From Val.

The full moon wasn't affecting him anymore; the constant buzz under his skin of high emotions waiting to be stoked to anger or desire had eased. But there was still a flip in his stomach when he saw Val's name on his screen. And maybe that warm, butterfly-soft feeling had been there before the past week and he just hadn't noticed it as much, but fuck, he was noticing it now.

He pressed his lips together as he opened the text, mentally preparing himself for Val to be establishing their boundaries firmly at just-friendship, but secretly hoping otherwise.

Hey Pup. I scheduled these texts for later in the day so it hopefully wouldn't wake you up too early. I don't know if you've opened the box yet. What's inside is vintage. I bought them in the early 80s, before I was turned, and then never wore them. They just didn't suit me. But they were expensive, so I hated to get rid of them.

When we were at Roseblood, the emeralds on the couch where we sat together reminded me of them, and I knew that I wanted to give them to you. They're partially a birthday gift, but mostly a thank-you. I could never have made it through last week without you, in more ways than one.

And I know we said we'd talk later, when our heads were clear. I'm not sure my head will ever be clear when it comes to you, but I'm ready to talk whenever you are.

Diego read the texts at least three more times before he finally put the phone down and flopped backward onto the creaky bed.

It was going to be a long fucking day until sunset.

EPILOGUE

It was the evening of November 2nd before Leland felt back to normal, which happened to be the day before Kimberly Fern had planned to go home.

"Think we can take her for breakfast tomorrow or something before she goes?" Leland asked Haley quietly while her mother was packing in the other room. "I feel bad that I never got to properly meet her. She just had to see me being sick and weird for a couple of days. Not sure I can overcome that first impression, but it'd be nice to make an effort."

Haley beamed at him and pushed up on her toes to kiss him. "I absolutely think we can talk her into breakfast first," she said warmly. "And I love that you asked."

Leland caught her with his hands on her hips, his thumbs rubbing over the soft curve of her waist, his favorite little roll there. "And...I know you said meeting your mom didn't have to be formal, or make anything official, or anything like that, and it's not like she doesn't already know, but..." He grimaced. "This is gonna sound awkward. I hadn't told anybody about us outside of town. The guys at work. My sister. I know you were worried about looking professional in the role, so I didn't want to mess that up. But it felt really weird on Halloween to act like we weren't together."

And he'd never admit it out loud, because it sounded exactly as pigheaded and ridiculous as it was, but it had bothered him to hear Walker talk about her, and he knew the other man would never have said it if he'd known Leland was dating her.

She was still looking at him expectantly, so he cleared his throat and took a deep breath. "So, I guess what I'm saying is...Haley Fern, will you be my girlfriend?"

"Um, *yes*?" Haley laughed and threw her arms around his neck and smacked another kiss against his lips. "I want you to know I wasn't offended. I figured you had your reasons. We do have a professional relationship, so I can imagine you might not want your boss to know how fast I managed to get you into bed."

He rolled her eyes at her teasing, and kissed the tip of her adorable, freckled nose, and the next day at breakfast, he made an extra effort to be polite to her mother and answer questions and try to make a good impression.

But eventually, Kimberly had to get on the road, so they wandered out into the parking lot, the two women still talking about something to do with werewolf policy or bylaws or something else he didn't quite understand. He was listening anyway and trying to keep up, but when he heard Prudence's special text tone, he abandoned the attempt and pulled his phone out of his pocket.

Two texts, in fact—one from Guerrera that he hadn't heard come in. *Niles showed back up. Apparently, his wife left him and he went on a week-long bender about it. Considering he didn't ask for the time off first, I think they might be going to take this opportunity to sack him. Fingers crossed.*

"I'll drink to that," Leland muttered to himself as he opened Prudence's text.

All right. I've applied to six colleges, including Montana State, in case you decide to stay there. I guess I won't know which ones I got into until March or April. I'll keep you updated.

He replied to Prudence with a thumbs-up and slid his phone back into his pocket in time to see Haley and Kimberly hug goodbye, and then Kimberly hesitated before she turned toward her car.

"Wait." Kimberly's fingers on the door of the car were white at the knuckles. "Before I go, there's something I... There's another reason I came back. I need to tell you something. I just...there wasn't a good time over the past few days and..."

Haley tilted her head in that way she had, her ponytail swishing across the back of her neck. "Are you okay, Mom? Are you...sick?"

"No, no, nothing like that. I'm fine. Everyone is fine."

Kimberly lifted her chin and squared her shoulders. The body language was familiar; Leland had seen it in Haley several times when she was winding up to do something that scared her. Leland stepped up behind Haley, one hand on her back; whatever Kimberly was about to say, he had a feeling Haley was going to need some support.

"The tribunal. In December." She took a deep breath. "Your father will be there."

***

Thank you for reading! Did you enjoy? Please add your review because nothing helps an author more and encourages readers to take a chance on a book than a review.

And don't miss more in the Moonrise series coming soon!

Until then read more paranormal romance like EMBERS by City Owl Author, Kat Turner. Turn the page for a sneak peek!

You can also sign up for the City Owl Press newsletter to receive notice of all book releases!

SNEAK PEEK OF EMBERS

By Kat Turner

Thom James couldn't pinpoint, with absolute certainty, when awareness of a void in his heart switched from minor nuisance to undeniable ache. On the latest routine morning in a long string, though, the abyss had stolen more than usual.

He pulled in a drag of cigarette smoke, the woodsy flavor more rote than satisfying as a rush of chemicals cancelled out the minty flavor of toothpaste. An exhale left his lungs in a choppy whoosh, his breath ejecting filmy gray residue. Here he was again, going through the motions.

He touched the cold glass of his hotel suite window and stared down at Nashville. Or Raleigh. Or perhaps his band had played Atlanta last night. Maybe they'd delivered their music to an arena of thirty-thousand cheering faces in Orlando or Dallas.

Didn't matter. This midsize city at morning was the same as any other: paper doll cutouts of buildings, drab redbrick and concrete tones, crumbling infrastructure. The theater of the mundane unfolded twenty stories below while he watched in a fruitless search for affect or even inspiration. A smattering of affordable cars lurched to jobs. A man wearing a backpack scurried down a sidewalk, prompting a cluster of pigeons to lift off in frantic flight.

Nearing the end of his forties and having played cities like this since his teen years, Thom had seen it all.

He'd felt the previous night, yes he had, high on the usual maelstrom of lust and fame.

At night, cities were sexy, glitter-sprinkled light shows teeming with promises, spectacles tailored to cater to the appetites. Come morning, though, they were little more than blight on the landscape. Interchangeable, half-real, used.

He spied a silver arch not far off in the distance, an artistic piece of architecture curving toward the clouds amid downtown buildings that weren't quite skyscrapers. Right, they'd played St. Louis the night before. That's where he was, not that it mattered.

A cynical bark of a laugh jumped out of his lips. Hollow mornings were the price he paid for his indulgent nights. The rock star's debt always came due.

From behind him came a soft, feminine moan. The bed squeaked, and the latest woman occupying whatever he called his bed sighed. The tomb in his chest gaped wider, a mocking reminder that a well-adjusted man would feel tender emotions right about now. His stomach tightened as his head spun. He stubbed out his smoke on the windowsill, snuffing his ennui.

Water rushed from the bathroom sink. Bodily noises of teeth getting scrubbed, gargling, and spitting followed. Thom smiled sadly. If their time together had been intended to be more than one night, the sounds of her freshening up might inspire intimate anticipation.

"Hey." Her voice, thick with sleep, belied a lilt of hope that toppled dominoes of guilt and regret inside him.

He turned to where she stood. A thin, white sheet swaddled her supple form, shielding the soft breasts that he'd enjoyed to the fullest. Her full-chest tattoo peeked out from the top of the material in coy glimpses of flowers crawling through emerald networks of jungle foliage.

His gaze travelled through the artwork on her chest and up to her lips, across freckled cheeks and northward to eyes as green as fresh-cut summertime grass. An inferno of chaotic red waves blazed past her shoulders.

She was quite pretty. Beautiful even, in an unconventional way with her strong features and robust bone structure. Ultimately, though, just another groupie. Another American woman in a city he couldn't place.

He didn't even know her name.

God, she deserved so much better than an empty fuck from the lowlife likes of him.

"Hi." He slid a piece of her hair through his fingers, appreciating the silkiness as he reminded himself not to be a dick. Quality aftercare in these situations kept his reputation sterling. "Sleep well?"

"Yeah. You knocked my ass out. I think it was that second orgasm that did me in. Or maybe the third. I'm pretty sure I'll have sweet dreams of the sexy British rocker for the rest of my life." With a siren's smirk, she snagged his pack of smokes off the nightstand and lit up.

Blowing rails through her nostrils, she jutted her chin in parry. Or defiance, daring him to condescend to her. Bloody hell. This bird was a live wire like none other, crackling with white heat.

Thom tilted his head to one side. Her brazenness, a shameless quality to her, piqued his intrigue. He slipped a finger into the swell of her cleavage and loosened the fabric concealing her breasts. "What's your name?"

She blew smoke in his face, the blast making him cough and blink as his eyes burned, though she didn't resist when her sheet fell to the floor. "You're an absolute pig." A touch of levity to her true statement betrayed affection. "Luckily for you, the accent *almost* makes up for it."

"You're still here. And naked again, I might add." Beneath his unbuttoned jeans, his prick swelled. He plucked the cigarette from her mouth, laid it in the ashtray, and guided her back to bed with two firm hands pushing against the velvety slopes of her shoulders.

"Touché." She walked backward in accordance with his motions, running slender fingers through the mat of hair covering his bare chest. The redhead flopped on the bed and spread her legs, her crooked smile both vulnerable and caustic. "I have a lot of problems."

His hands were busy attacking his zipper when fresh waves of shame and disgust pummeled him. Christ, what was wrong with him, screwing women as if they were mere objects? What a scoundrel he was.

"I'm so sorry." He slashed a hand through his hair, the strands as unkempt as the rest of his life, and pulled his thick mess into a ponytail in some pitifully symbolic effort to order his chaos. "Are you hungry? I can have some room service sent up if you'd prefer discretion, but if you'd like to go out, that's fine too. Or I can call you a car if you're ready to get out of here."

Her smile spread while she appraised him with a knowing, green-eyed gaze. "You don't need to pay me with food. I'm a slut, not a whore. Nothing against whores, but judge me correctly." Though she spoke in a jesting tone, her words cut like a scalpel.

She hadn't closed her legs—gorgeous pink pussy, trimmed strip of red hair—but now Thom wasn't sure if he felt aroused, embarrassed, ashamed, or some unwholesome mix of all three. He stood there blinking like an idiot, his face hot and a nest of brown pubes sprouting through his open fly while a spotlight shone on his mortified conscience.

"You aren't either one of those." He stammered, his mouth dry. Though he meant what he said—his promiscuous arse had no right to pass judgment—the words came off forced and ridiculous. "You're a beautiful person. I wished I would have gotten to know you a little better before we ended up naked."

He meant that too. Yet some unseen force stopped him, time and again, from seeking out a deeper level of intimacy with women. It was easier to approach them as empty conquests.

Easier to forget them. Easier to keep his emotional wall high and solid.

She smacked her forehead. "A beautiful person? That's the cringiest platitude I've ever heard. Can we please fuck? I don't need to witness you thumping every branch on the way down to rock bottom."

Tension and self-consciousness flew out of him in an inexplicable gust. For all his cavorting and playing the part of boorish lout, Thom never quite felt at ease or at peace. He envied the woman on the bed, how she lay there open and free, unshaken.

"Nice metaphor." He swiped the half-burned cigarette out of the ashtray, drew down a hit, and handed the smoke to his temporary partner. "Were you an English major?" She had to be in her mid-thirties and was articulate enough to be a college grad.

Her ample chest swelled as she partook, falling when she blew out three wobbly smoke rings. He studied the multicolor splash of ink capping her breasts and marveled at the way those inquisitive eyes of hers tracked the vapory hoops as they floated before dissipating. "I'm an English professor."

He sat next to her on the bed, and she scooted over to accommodate. Considering her cue, he trailed three kisses from her shoulder to her collarbone, seeking her scent. Floral and spicy notes mixed with her tang from below. Her exotic scent suited her perfectly, even in the stark light of day. "That's sexy. Will you read to me?"

"Why, can't you read?"

For the first time, he noticed precise details of her voice. Beneath the smokiness and snark lay a melody. She spoke like a song, her rhythm rising and falling. Thom buried his face in her neck, sampling her flesh with teasing flicks of his tongue. She whined a little pleasure noise, and with that he was stiff as a bat again. "Tell me your name. Please."

"No. It's more fun this way. Anonymous."

He urged his cock from his pants and rubbed the swollen head against the soft expanse of her outer thigh, seeking relief from the pressure building in his lower belly.

"Well, you're anonymous to me, sweetheart. I'm a famous bassist, and you know exactly who I am."

The feel of his own hot breath against her skin, the arrogant truth of his cocky words, made boiling cum swirl in his balls. Sure, he got off on his own fame, notoriety, and status. No fool would dare nominate him for sainthood.

"Your ego is out of control." She punched her hips up, and he took the cue and danced teasing fingertips down her smooth stomach. "And I actually don't know you. Right now I have the idea of you, the fantasy. Which is precisely what I want."

"Fair enough." His pulse accelerated. Blood fled his brain and filled his engorged cock. As his eyes feasted upon his partner's inviting form, he took a moment to admire the length and girth of his impressive member, the healthy purple coloring of the swollen tip. He could not wait to feed this luscious, vexing piece of feminine excellence to his hungry beast.

But for now, her pleasure was his priority. Thom might be a cad, but at least he left his bedmates with fond memories of his skills. "What do you want me to do, love? Finger you? Eat you? Rub my dick over your clit?"

"Damn, I'm all about your dirty talk." Her thighs quivered, the musky smell of her arousal intensifying.

He played with the soft curls on her mound, kneeling between her legs to admire her swollen folds and the visible bulge of her sensitive nub. He sunk two fingers inside her, licking his lips at the first touch of pussy, a tease of what his prick wanted so bad. In smooth motions, he moved those two fingers in and out, every ounce of his being committed to holding off on the raging urge to plunge inside of her and take, take, take.

"Yeah," she said, eyes glazed and lips parted.

"You want me to use my fingers?" His rod flexed, a bead of pre-cum leaking out.

Driving women crazy with his talents made him feel like a god. The potent rush of ego beat a quick one-off any day.

"Please." She sat up, her eyelids and pale lashes hooding her eyes when her gaze fell to the piston work of his hand.

"Jesus, I can see your clit. I can see how big and full it is, ripe." He withdrew from her opening and used the two slick fingers to spread her folds, making a V through which the glistening button popped like a red candy apple.

She moaned a reply and began to pinch and rub her own stiff nipples.

"I'm going to stroke your clit now, slowly with my thumb. I don't want you to come too fast, but you're so round and red I don't know if I'll be able to prolong your climax. Forgive me."

Another unintelligible grunt from Ms. Articulate English Professor. Christ, this was fun.

He'd circle back to this very moment every time he felt a flare of remorse about how freely he fucked around.

He brought the pad of his thumb to her target, admiring the smooth, slick feel of the bump as he stroked in a big circle. A few passes around, and her clit went into spasms. She lost control, bucking and moaning as she came apart.

Using his opposite hand, Thom slid a finger back into her, hooking his digit on her equally flush G-spot, and rubbed methodically. Her inner muscles clenched and released all around his plunges, her body's responses proof of orgasm.

With a sharp cry, she froze. Her eyes stretched wide, and her jaw dropped. "Oh fuck, I'm coming."

"You sure are." Once she was done, he grabbed his dick and stroked up and down, slowly, offering a little show. "You ready for more?"

"Hell yes."

"Ah, give me that fiery red pussy, baby." With an unbridled growl, he fell on her and plunged inside her pocket of warm, liquid heaven. She'd sworn last night that she was on the pill, and he trusted that she was telling the truth.

Firm walls molded around his cock, sucking like hungry mouths as he mindlessly thrust in and out. "Goddamn, that's some bloody good snatch." He cupped one of her large breasts, pumping hard and fast in selfish pursuit of release.

"Thanks." She wrapped her legs around his hips and dragged her trimmed nails down his back. "I take good care of it. Only the best."

A laugh, this one earnest and bereft of the poison of cynicism, sprang from his lips. A weird, bubbly sensation cavorted in Thom, unnerving but not unwelcome. He slowed his strokes and gazed deeply into his partner's pretty eyes. "Does this feel good?"

"Yes," she whispered, squeezing his shoulders. His lover smiled at him, and the bubbles in his chest and abdomen swelled larger.

He kissed the tip of her nose before resuming his work, taking care this time to angle his pelvis so the root of his shaft connected with her clit when he withdrew on the down stroke.

When she began to moan again and her walls tightened and released in time, Thom closed his eyes and savored her. Her smell, her sounds, the comforts of her softness and sex. A lump lodged in his throat, and the inside of his nose stung. He'd never made love, but perhaps his current experience of the sex act amounted to a poor man's version.

"Thom, you're so good." She fell limp.

Before he could think too much about those false words she spoke and what it would mean for them to become true, he sped his plunges to the frantic, needy pace required to bring him home.

Her eyes darkened into a dirty, sinful stare. "You're about to come. Your balls are high and tight now, huh? Full of a big load you can't wait to blow."

"You're so fucking hot I can't stand it." He clutched her tit, his skin tingling as he rushed to the end. Base, unspeakable need overcame him, the tension below his waist ratcheting to a fiendish craving.

"Come all over me."

Heat unspooled near the base of his shaft. He gaped at the spot where their bodies joined, marveling at the wonder of his prick slipping in and out, his rigid flesh coated with the glisten of her juices. The second relief tore in, he pulled out and gave three final tugs right below the ridge of the head.

Thom cried out while he splintered into shocks of ecstasy. Blank and blissed with awestruck emptiness, he gawked as thick white ropes splashed her breasts, hair, and cheek.

"Fuck." Aftershocks reverberated through his body. He rubbed his stomach and squeezed his still-stiff member until the final drops of fluid eked out and dripped onto her chest.

"Now lick it off me and feed it back into my mouth."

"Pardon?" He struggled to regulate his breathing, clobbered by the double whammy of a life-erasing orgasm and her request. No woman had ever asked *that* of him.

"You heard me."

Lost in the haze of her thrall, he obeyed, scooping up his own bittersweet semen with eager lips and tongue. When he took her mouth, he forgot all about the nasty, kinky deed and melted into their first kiss.

And what a first kiss it was.

Her effort was predictably assertive, skilled from practice, though more sensual than he would have guessed. But as their tongues stroked, played, gave, and took in a series of caresses and lazy searching, a frighteningly glorious thought sunk hooks into Thom's mind and heart.

I could get used to this.

"Oh, shit." She broke the kiss with a start and lunged for a bedside table, grimacing when she palmed her wristwatch.

"What's wrong? Are you alright?" He reached for her, overcome by an irrational worry that he'd bolloxed something up and caused her to hate him. Absurd that he cared, because if she hated him, she'd leave without a fuss.

She shook her head while bending over, her pale and naked bottom a curvaceous temptation dangling just outside his reach. Last night's clothes flew onto the bed—the red bustier, black leather miniskirt, and matching jacket she'd worn to the Chariotz of Fyre after-party where they'd met. "I missed my flight."

Her body in that outfit had turned his head hard and made his tongue wag with an unspeakable urge to have her. But by now, he ought to have been feeling profound relief when faced with her impending departure.

As his nameless lover shimmied and wiggled into her clothing, the reality of her slipping away lanced him. He glanced at his hands, then the floor. *I do not want to lose her*, Thom thought with an odd and startling clarity.

Normally, he lost interest in a woman after the two of them had had their fill of sex and laughs. Yet here he was moping like a schoolboy in puppy love when he damn well ought to be thanking the good lord above that the groupie of the day was about to bolt without tears, begging, or his insistence. "Can I help?"

"No." She took a cell phone from her purse and rang someone while sliding her pretty feet into danger heels.

"What's up, Megan?" A faint male voice spoke through the line.

Thom clenched his teeth and glowered at a random spot on the wall. Megan. The stupid bloke on the phone got to know her name, but he didn't. What had this wanker done that Thom hadn't to earn the privilege?

"I'm so sorry, Gary, but I'm gonna be late for the setup tonight. I travelled to St. Louis for a work thing, and I missed my flight out. I'm going to rent a car and jet up there right now, so if the drive goes okay, I'll be onsite in time to help with equipment."

What sort of equipment did an English professor need? If he'd conversed with her in more depth than his usual flirtatious small talk allowed for, the context would have meant something. Since he hadn't tried, though, he got to sit on the bed as a clueless outsider, cursing his thoughtlessness and stupidity.

Worse, he was nothing to her. Less than nothing. He was a lie, a "work thing." Served him right, he supposed. She was using him just like he'd assumed that he was using her. Karma was having a right-and-proper point and laugh moment.

Megan popped open a tin of mints and tossed three in her mouth before chucking the box in her bag. "Thanks for everything, stud."

She dropped a chaste kiss to his cheek, a literal kiss-off. He actually felt himself shrink.

He caught her fingers and thought fast. "It's already noon, and the sun goes down so early this month. Please, let me arrange a flight for you." That way he'd learn of her destination, her home state.

"It's only a five-hour drive to Iowa from here. I'll be fine." Glancing at the door, she slung her purse high on her shoulder.

Iowa. Noted. Megan the English professor from Iowa. Might be able to piece a puzzle together from those scraps. College departments had directories with pictures, and with any luck, there was a syllabus floating around out there somewhere with her cell number on it. "Why the rush? Aren't most universities still closed for the holiday?"

Though he'd graduated college over two decades ago, he hadn't forgotten about the existence of a winter break.

"Oh, I'm not going home for my professor job. I have a side gig." She slipped free of his hold and made haste for the exit.

"What's that?" He laid his empty hand to rest on the mattress, clinging to the phantom sensation of her final touch.

"I'm a paranormal investigator. And just so you're aware, when we were at the party I detected a negative entity or presence near your band. I don't say this to scare you, but you may want to think about getting in contact with someone who deals in exorcisms. Thanks again for last night and this morning. Bye."

Before he could ask the first of about a hundred questions invading his confused, vaguely horrified thoughts, Megan dipped out and shut the door behind her.

Don't stop now. Keep reading with your copy of EMBERS by City Owl Author, Kat Turner.

And find more from Jules Kelley at julesrobinkelley.com

Want even more paranormal romance? Try EMBERS by City Owl Author, Kat Turner, and find more from Jules Kelley at julesrobinkelley.com

Thom James is tired of his wild but empty rock star life, so when he meets a fan who is as uninhibited and unapologetic as he is, he falls hard. Problem is, she's busy chasing ghosts and has no interest in a serious relationship. Before she says goodbye, the enigmatic groupie leaves Thom with a dire warning about dark forces that are attached to his band.

Freshly fired from her professor job, Megan O'Neil is strictly focused on pouring herself into her side gig: ghost hunting. She can't get her latest hookup out of her mind, though, and her connection to notorious rocker Thom James inconveniently persists when she forgets her demon-trapping watch in his hotel room. When he tracks her down to return the lost object, she confronts her growing feelings for the famous bassist along with a realization that she must tackle a nasty curse that's way above her pay grade. Too bad the curse, which has followed her since childhood, is not about to be neutralized without a fight.

Now, Thom and Megan must battle not only a malevolent spirit, but a fierce attraction that feels doomed by the demands of their incompatible lives. When Megan excavates a strange book of witchcraft and taps into a world of magic with ties to a terrifying prophecy, she and Thom face down not only the challenges of making a relationship work, but of somehow halting the machinery of magical fate before everyone pays the price.

Please sign up for the City Owl Press newsletter for chances to win special subscriber-only contests and giveaways as well as receiving information on upcoming releases and special excerpts.

All reviews are **welcome** and **appreciated**. Please consider leaving one on your favorite social media and book buying sites.

Escape Your World. Get Lost in Ours! City Owl Press at www.cityowlpress.com.

ACKNOWLEDGMENTS

Thanks are owed to Saritza Hernandez and my editor, Tee Tate, for their support and patience while multiple health issues quite literally plagued my efforts to finish this book; to my wife, who offered encouragement in a dozen little ways; and to Cecilia Tan for tarot-ing and talking me through a plot crisis. And last but not least, my sincere gratitude to Kelsey Allagood whose vocal adoration of Diego Sanchez gave me the determination to make it through.

ABOUT THE AUTHOR

JULES KELLEY is an author of self-described "cozy spec fic," exploring what the ordinary looks like in extraordinary settings and finding the common ground between them. Her hobbies are whatever her ADHD is hyperfixating on at the time, but make it queer. She has a weakness for scented candles, vintage aesthetics, and rescue animals, including the two that live with her and her wife in central Florida. Find more about her at julesrobinkelley.com and Tumblr at juleskelleybooks.tumblr.com

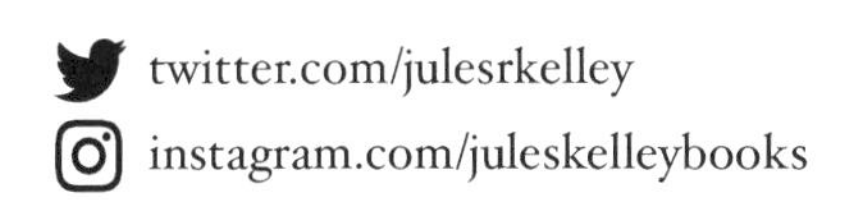

ABOUT THE PUBLISHER

City Owl Press is a cutting edge indie publishing company, bringing the world of romance and speculative fiction to discerning readers.

Escape Your World. Get Lost in Ours!

www.cityowlpress.com

facebook.com/YourCityOwlPress
twitter.com/cityowlpress
instagram.com/cityowlbooks
pinterest.com/cityowlpress

Made in the USA
Columbia, SC
18 April 2023